**Dot to Dot - Text copyright © Emmy Ellis 2019
Cover Art by Emmy Ellis @ studioenp.com © 2019**

All Rights Reserved

Dot to Dot is a work of fiction. All characters, places, and events are from the author's imagination. Any resemblance to persons, living or dead, events or places is purely coincidental.

The author respectfully recognises the use of any and all trademarks.

With the exception of quotes used in reviews, this book may not be reproduced or used in whole or in part by any means existing without written permission from the author.

Warning: The unauthorised reproduction or distribution of this copyrighted work is illegal. No part of this book may be scanned, uploaded, or distributed via the Internet or any other means, electronic or print, without the author's written permission.

DOT TO DOT

EMMY ELLIS

ACKNOWLEDGEMENTS

Thank you to the following people for allowing me to use their names as I saw fit:

Mike Redmond, Sara Scott, Gabby Raines, Michelle Bradbury, Rona Danridge, Toni Morin

PROLOGUE

Maybe he should have waited. Talked to her a bit more. Given her a chance to explain her behaviour. She might not be like *her* at all and he'd just imagined it. The thing was, he was tired of being confused, always had been. She never failed to get her own way in the end—he gave in and agreed that *Yes, you're right.*

Yes, I was wrong. Yes, you can run roughshod over me, no matter how I feel about it.

As a kid, he'd learnt to do as *she* said.

He was sick of it.

Mike stood beside the bed, staring down at his girlfriend, Olivia. She'd stayed over, a rare occurrence, as she preferred her own bed, in her own house, in her own perfect world. She didn't like him staying over at hers. He had to leave when she was ready to go to sleep.

She snored gently, mouth slightly parted, eyelashes resting on her skin, long and a tad curled. He'd thought her pretty once, but then she'd changed and showed her true colours. That always seemed to happen, didn't it. Someone was attractive, and the minute their real self was revealed, they became ugly all round, even if their face was beautiful.

He held out his gloved hands—shaking, they were—and flexed his fingers, ready to do the business. Olivia stirred, mumbling something, probably berating him in her dreams, standing there pointing her finger, waggling it.

Anger burned, and Mike ran his tongue over his teeth, back and forth, a soothing action he'd done forever. Olivia didn't like it. Said it got on her nerves. That he looked like a loser doing it.

That had been the wrong thing to say.

"What the fuck are you *doing*, Mike?" she snapped.

He jolted, had lost concentration for a second there, and leant over to kiss her cheek to disguise him picking up his tool that he slid in his pocket.

"I'm off out to walk the dog. She's whining for a wee."

"Manky thing should be put in a shelter," she muttered and rolled over, her back to him.

She shouldn't say shit like that about his dog. That had been Olivia's mistake from the start. She reckoned Dot was smelly, that the poor old girl shouldn't be allowed to have accidents on the lino from time to time. And she definitely shouldn't be allowed on the sofa. Well, Dot had been with Mike for a damn sight longer than Olivia, and guess which bitch would get to stay in his life? Not the one in front of him, he knew that much.

His chance to get rid of her over, he scratched his bald head and left the room, went downstairs and woke Dot, who wiggled her tail and whimpered at the sound of the chain on her lead tinkling.

"Come on, my lovely. Let's go and see what we can find."

He stepped out into a frosty, dark early morning, ice sparkling on the drive beneath the light of the lamppost. Three a.m. was pretty murky in winter, wasn't it, and his neighbours were used to him coming in and out at odd hours, what with his job and him being on call sometimes. So with his behaviour nothing for anyone to be concerned about, he walked past three houses, then entered the alley between two. It led to the garages out the back, and while Dot was having a piddle on a patch of grass at the edge of the tarmac, he got his car out ready for a bit of a jaunt.

He whistled quietly, and Dot padded over, climbing into the back seat with a little help from Mike. He drove out of the garage area and took a right, coming out into Bluebird Avenue where he always put his work van, then through the estate, out onto the main road, and then to Peacock Lane. He parked up, took his pouch from the glove box, and placed his tool in it. He left Dot in the car with her blankie and strode over to the skinny detached houses, his breath clouding, cold nipping his nose.

It was a scabby area, on the verge of getting CCTV, but all was quiet now, even the drug pushers in bed. The woman he used to visit for *you know what* lived in the first on the left. She'd now be dead before Olivia…and after *her*.

He shoved thoughts of *her* away. His mum. She'd been a bitch an' all.

Mike took the key from where it was wedged behind the back of the wall-mounted postbox, one of those black fancy efforts with a slot and a silver lock, the word MAIL on it in gold font, like people wouldn't know what it was for. The council houses on Peacock Lane had had their doors changed recently. Letterboxes weren't good here. Someone was going round putting lit paper through them. People had died. *Dogs* had died. That bit had upset Mike the most. The thought of them howling…

No. Mustn't. Don't imagine or remember.

He let himself into Sara's, mindful of the doormat. It sometimes slipped on the laminate. She kept meaning to buy one of those grip things to put underneath, and it was clear she still hadn't. He skidded, righting himself by gripping the jamb.

Good job he'd kept his gloves on, wasn't it.

"Who's that?" Sara called from upstairs, her tone giving away the fact she was groggy.

He'd bet she slept light these days, always alert, what with the fires going on. Sensible really. You never knew who could turn up in the middle of the night, did you.

Smile.

Mike closed the door and climbed the stairs, slipping his pouch in his pocket. "It's me," he said at her bedroom doorway. The lamp was on, a low watt that only lit the immediate surroundings, throwing everything else into shadow.

"It had to be either you or Ted, maybe Jacob."

Her voice, full of sleep, annoyed him. Or maybe it was the reminder that he wasn't, and never had been, the only man in her life. She wasn't *that* sort of woman, the kind you had to pay, and he'd known from the start she had another two on the go other than him, but still, he'd thought he could be her one and only, get her to like him more than Ted or Jacob. Turned out he hadn't, and he shouldn't have been surprised. He hadn't manged to get Mum to like him more than anyone else either, and he'd tried so hard to do that.

Once he'd met Olivia, visits to Sara had been few and far between, but he'd come from time to time, to check whether she'd ditched the other two blokes and was prepared to just love him.

There was having hope, then there was blatant stupidity.

"Haven't seen you for ages," Sara said, the quilt a bundle of blue over her body. "Things not going well with the girlfriend?"

"No." He walked in and stood beside the bed. Stared down at her like he'd stared at Olivia. Saw Olivia, saw Mum. They all looked the same. Brown hair with a tint of red if the light caught it a certain way. Hazel eyes. Slim noses.

They could be mistaken for being related.

I hate you all.

I love you all.

That horrible confusion crept in. He detested it. How could you love and hate at the same time?

"What's going on with her then?" Sara gazed up at him, sleepy dust in the corner of her eye.

Mike nearly lost it. Why did memories have a habit of creeping out when you didn't want them to? Why did he now see her as Mum, that day when— "She's mean, like my mother."

"Oh. Not good."

No, it wasn't, and really, he shouldn't be here, with Sara, doing what he was about to do. He hadn't even planned to come here, well, not so soon anyway. So far, it had all been scribbles in his A4 pad, years of them. And Sara had been nice to him, so kind, and the only thing she had in the negative column was having the misfortune to resemble his mother.

"I'm sorry," he said, those words a staple in his childhood.

"What for?" Sara frowned.

"For this…"

CHAPTER ONE

Olivia woke and checked the clock. Mike's was really annoying, with massive numbers about four inches high that lit the room up. She preferred sleeping in total darkness. Quite a bit of time had passed since she'd caught him staring down at her in that weird way of his, and he still wasn't back in bed. That Dot had a lot to answer for. She took up far too much of Mike's time and affection, when it should be Olivia he doted on the most—not that she wanted him to dote on her.

He'd mumbled something once, and she hadn't understood it.

"Dot to dot, that's what it's been. Going from one dot to another," he'd said.

Must have been to do with his scabby mutt, but it'd bugged her when he hadn't explained what he'd meant. Kept saying she'd find out soon enough and to wait, because surprises were always better when sprung on you. He told her about the first puppy he'd got, how great *that* surprise had been, so he knew she'd enjoy it when he gave her one.

Now she came to think of it, a few things bugged her about Mike. Like how he stared at her sometimes, his eyes all glassy, fists clenched. It was as if he went into a trance where nobody else existed. Or when he'd insisted she used wet wipes on her eyes if she'd been asleep. He wouldn't look at her until she'd done it, got rid of any sleepy dust. Then there was the bizarre thing he did with his teeth. He licked them, lips pulled back, and this strange sound rumbled in his throat. Sounded like Dot when she'd been constipated that time.

What am I still doing with him?

He was supposed to have been a stopgap, someone to fill the void between serious boyfriends, except he'd *become* a serious boyfriend—well, he thought he had anyway, but she'd made up her mind to finish with him today.

Last night had been the final hurrah. Someone else had expressed an interest, and because she hadn't told anyone she was seeing Mike—she was ashamed, to be honest; he was a bit of a geek, not her usual type at all—it had been easy to accept the offer of a dinner date from Frankie, her next-door neighbour. She should have known it was time to finish with Mike when she'd found out he liked doing those dot-to-dot puzzles, the freak.

She got up, fucked off at being awake so early on a Sunday. After a shower, she dressed then shoved her toothbrush and whatnot in her bag. She'd have a coffee—who could start the day properly without it?—break the news to Mike, then go to the café for a slap-up breakfast. Celebrate having no ties. Until she got with Frankie, that was. He was right up her alley. Good-looking, a bit of all right as the girls at work had said after Olivia had shown them his picture on Facebook.

Downstairs, she put her bag on the kitchen table and stuck a pod in the coffee machine, setting it to pour. Dot wasn't on her smelly, hair-infested bed in the corner, so she might be in the living room on the sofa with Mike. Disgusting. While the coffee created spurting noises and the scent floated out, she stomped in to see if her suspicions were correct.

No Mike. No dog.

Where the hell was he? Did he *really* need to spend hours walking that ancient bag of bones?

She flounced back to the kitchen, stopping short at the sound of the key going in the lock. She spun and faced the front door at the end of the hallway, Mike's shape visible though the leaf-patterned glass. He stepped inside, head bent, a bulging black bin liner in his hand. Christ, did the dog shit that much?

Dot dashed into the kitchen then skidded to a halt upon seeing Olivia. The animal whined her seriously irritating whine, backing out into the hallway with Mike, who looked up.

He had blood on his face.

Olivia's heart clattered. Maybe he'd caught himself on a briar. Dot liked to go to a little forest up the way, so Mike had probably brushed past a tree branch. It must have been one with a fair few thorns or whatever, as he had four slashes down one cheek.

"What are you doing up?" He closed the door quietly and placed the bin liner on the floor.

"Thought I may as well go home, seeing as you weren't here." She moved backwards to get her coffee.

Dot scuttled in on her gangly legs, scampering off to her bed as though Olivia was about to wallop her or something. Her skittish behaviour really was ridiculous. Olivia bit back a spiteful barb and sipped her drink. Mike came in, pulling his black gloves off, and placed them on the draining board. Was that blood on the white stitching of the pointer finger? It seemed like it, soaked into the end, as though he'd used it to wipe it from his face.

"I see you hurt yourself then." She leant her arse against the worktop.

He was doing that glazed eyes thing, his hands in tight balls, knuckles white, jaw clenched, his focus on the kitchen window, which, with the light on, reflected his weird-as-fuck stare. A long, single strand of hair was draped over the shoulder of his jacket, the same colour as hers, brown with a hint of red.

She studied his cheek. The blood was crusting, as if the scratches had only recently stopped bleeding. Some blood had smudged, giving his skin a pink hue. She drank more of her coffee, waiting for his statue phase to pass. It usually did after a minute or two. She'd got used to it, but it didn't mean she liked it. Anyway, she wouldn't have to see it anymore once her cup was empty, and thank heavens for that.

Olivia switched her attention to Dot. She was an Irish Wolfhound, all wiry fur in different shades of grey. The animal gazed at her from the bed, chin flat on it between her paws, the whites around her eyes showing. Why was she so afraid all the time? The only one she didn't act nervous around was Mike. He'd said once that he had a bond with Dot, more than he'd had with any human. Well, Dot was welcome to him. Mike wasn't all that good in the sack anyway, so she wouldn't miss *that*. Like she'd said, stopgap. A girl had to take what she could get when the well ran dry.

Coffee done with, she placed the cup in the washing-up bowl. Looked at Mike's reflection. He wasn't with it at all. She turned and faced him. Patted his arm to pull him out of his trance. Where did he go when he did that? What was he thinking about? He never had told her. Said it was his business.

Mike blinked. Shook his head.

"Listen." She grabbed her bag, hung it over her shoulder. "We're not working. I'm going to call it a day. Find someone else." She held her breath, waiting for him to give some kind of reaction. She waited a full minute. "What, no asking me why? No fighting to stay together?"

He stared.

"Okay, then consider us finished. Enjoy finding someone to put up with your skanky animal. Oh, and if it's her who slashed your face, she needs her claws clipping and a smack on the nose to teach her to behave herself."

She strutted to the front door, wondering if Mike would ask her to come back, plead with her to stay, that they could work it out.

Nothing.

Olivia opened the door an inch or so, telling herself it was just as well he hadn't kicked up a fuss. She couldn't be doing with histrionics, and it proved her decision was the right one if he wasn't bothered. She'd wasted far too much time on him already. Door open farther, she made to move back so she could get out, but something blocked her. She glanced to the side and caught sight of Mike in her peripheral. God, was he going to cuddle her from behind, beg her not to leave? Really, she wasn't in the bloody mood.

"It's no good, Mike," she said. "Hugs won't change my mind."

"I'm sorry," he said.

"What, for being a shit lover?"

"No, for what I'm going to do."

"What's that then?"

"Doesn't matter."

"Right, well... If you could just step back, that'd be great."

He did, and she walked out, off round the back to where she'd left her car in the space closest to Mike's garage. That was odd. When she'd arrived last night, his hadn't been out, but there it was, parked in front of the garage door. Curiosity got the better of her, and she touched the bonnet. Warm. So it *had* been as she'd thought. He'd taken his precious Dot to the forest.

Shrugging, she took a step or two, and something on the passenger seat gave her pause. What was that? Hard to tell in the dark, and there were no security lamps in this area. She opened her door so the interior light splashed out. Threw her bag on the back seat. Then she peered inside Mike's. One of those old-fashioned peg dolls lay on the seat, the round ball at the top its head. A crude face had been drawn on it with what might be a black Sharpie, and it had brown wool for hair.

Like mine.

She shivered off that thought and checked the rest of it out. It had a dress on of sorts, this weird Aztec pattern in oranges, reds, and yellows. Fuzzy pipe cleaners stuck out for arms, and was that pink plasticine balls for hands? What the hell did he want an ugly thing like that for? It was weird, creepy, and she was doubly glad she'd finished with him now. Who knew what he was really like deep down?

A shudder crept up her spine, and she glanced around, sensing someone watching her. At the bottom of the area were the row of houses in Mike's street, but trees grew so high she couldn't see them through the evergreens. Anyone could be standing in front of the wooden fences behind them, and she wouldn't know. Quickly, she got in her car, slamming the door then reaching for the seat belt. Something brushed her fingers, soft fabric, fleece, and she stared at the passenger side. A shape sat there, a *person* shape, and she opened her mouth to scream. Whoever it was clamped a palm over it and dug their gloved fingertips into her cheek.

She snorted through her nose, lifted her fist to punch in the vicinity of the shadow face, but they gripped her wrist with their other hand.

"Calm down."

Fuck, fuck, is that Mike?

God, she'd bloody kill him.

"You treated me like shit, Peggy," he said.

Peggy? Who the chuff was that? She shook her head, a massive worm of unease wriggling in her chest. Mike didn't sound right, not his usual, quiet-voiced self, and she didn't like it. She wanted to tell him to get out but instead brought her other arm up to claw at his face. It hit her, right then, with startling clarity, where he'd got those marks on his cheek.

He'd done this before.

"It's time to go." He pressed his hand harder over her lips. "You're going to drive us to your house. I have a knife in my pocket, and if you don't go straight there, I'll stab you with it."

Christ, if she'd known he'd take their breakup like this, she'd have done it in a public place, in daylight. Maybe he cared more than she'd thought. To react like this, though... He wasn't right in the head.

"I'm going to move my hand away from your nasty little gob, Peggy, so I can show you the knife. You'll know I mean it then. You'll keep quiet. You won't try to hurt me. You've hurt me enough, and I won't stand for it anymore. Like they say, you can only kick a dog so many times before they bite. Dot bit you, and you realised then, didn't you."

Dot hadn't bitten her at all, so what he was going on about, Olivia didn't know. Regardless, she nodded to let him know she'd behave, and she would, until she got home. Then she'd get away from him, ring the police, and have his insane arse arrested.

He removed his palm, and she pulled in a long breath. He switched the interior light on and withdrew a knife from his jacket pocket, the one he used to cut cheese. It had two points on the end, a snake's tongue, and glinted as he moved it from side to side.

She scrabbled to open her door with her free hand, and he lunged across to pin her to the seat.

"Not a good idea. Now get a move on." He let her wrist go, pointing the blade at her, and switched the light off.

Shaking and in no fit state to drive, she managed to get her keys out of her pocket and slide them in the ignition. While she manoeuvred a shaky reverse from her spot, she thought of ways she could alert someone she was trapped in her car with a nutter—without him knowing what she was doing. The problem was, it was dark, so if she flashed her headlights, he'd see her silent cry for help. If she tapped her foot on the brake a few times, he'd notice that, too. And with it being so early, and a Sunday morning, most people's usual day for having a lie-in, there wouldn't be anyone on the roads anyway.

Maybe she could fling herself out while the car was in motion. It'd crash, and she could run away.

She coasted out onto Bluebird Avenue, her chest constricting. His heavy breathing beside her sent her legs weak, and she willed herself to remain calm. Once she arrived in her street she'd scream, fuck waiting to get her phone out and call the police.

But your phone's in your bag. On the back seat.
Oh God.

The journey home so far was the weirdest she'd ever experienced. Tense. The air steeped with the buzz of fear. Several times she told herself to get out or do an emergency stop so he shot forward and banged his head. She didn't, though.

Olivia trembled, her body cold, her teeth chattering. He didn't speak, just breathed, loud and fast, as if he was angry or excited, she couldn't work out which. She snatched glimpses of him from the corner of her eye, the streetlamps giving her a better view. His torso was still twisted, him facing her, that knife at a level with the vulnerable soft flesh of her side. She imagined the blade slicing through her hoody and into her skin, wishing she hadn't. The urge to go to the toilet came on suddenly, and she held in a whimper at the pain streaking through her bladder.

Almost at her place, he said, "Park down the side of your house."

She jumped, having got used to just the sound of his breathing, and a small cry floated out of her.

"When we get out, go round the back."

He was well aware, like at his, the trees at the bottom of her garden would prevent anyone in the houses behind from seeing them creep across to her back door. She lived in a detached two-bed, so she couldn't even bang on the internal walls of next door and wake Frankie up. Their driveways created too much space for her to run over there, and there was a low wall between them. Mike would be on her inside a second, hauling her back, maybe by her hair.

She drove down her street, frantically checking the houses for signs of people being awake. All the curtains appeared to be closed, and no lights were on inside the properties. She couldn't think if it was number fifteen's week to be up early for work—sometimes, he slammed his car door about this time and didn't seem to care if he woke anyone up.

Turning into her drive was the hardest thing she'd ever had to do—knowing Mike had something horrible in store for her and not being able to do a thing about it. She parked at an angle where he'd told her and waited. Stared ahead at where the tarmac led straight onto her back garden grass, her wheelie bins, one blue, one green, standing beside the fence between hers and Frankie's. Could she climb on them, vault over, and hammer on his door? Mike might run away then, worried about being caught.

"Stay there until I get to the other side and let you out. Open your door." Mike left the car.

She obeyed him, her door flying open, then shoved the gear stick in reverse and prepared to escape. But he didn't go around the front as she'd expected. She caught a flash of him in the side mirror, standing by her boot, all looming and tall and frightening, and her first chance of escape fizzled to nothing—she didn't have the balls to run him over despite what he'd put her through.

"Oh fuck, oh fuck…" She darted her gaze around to find something to attack him with. Nothing. Key yanked out of the ignition, she clutched the bunch in her hand and poked one key between two fingers, a knife of her own, albeit one that wouldn't do that much damage unless she managed to poke him in the eye or through his cheek, maybe his neck.

Then he was there, at her door, his hand coming inside to grip her hoody and drag her from the vehicle. She raised her fist to stab him, but he blocked the upwards momentum with his wrist.

I dropped the fucking keys.

A wretched sound burbled out of her mouth, and a sense of impending doom settled over her.

She'd have to comply until she got to the wheelie bins. That was her next chance at breaking free. The cold air snaked beneath the neckline of her hoody, and he dragged her away from the door and shut it. Marched her down the last bit of the drive. She side-eyed him, and he glared ahead, so, with the assurance he wasn't watching her, she opened her mouth and took a deep breath and—

The side of his fist holding the knife bashed into her lips, her nose. Eyes watering, pain sparking, she choked out a pain-filled sob, and he yanked her around the corner and into her garden. Shoved her against the wall beside the kitchen window.

"Now, Peggy, you're going to keep your fucking mouth shut and do as you're told." His hot breath hit her chin. "It's about time you did."

CHAPTER TWO

Tracy had the whole day planned—doing a lot of sod all. She'd get Damon's arse out of bed in a minute with the scent of bacon, and they'd become people, not a DI and a DS. She was tired from a recent case and needed to remove herself from her job for today, not only physically but mentally. Days on end spent steeped in an investigation took its toll. Weekends were for fun—if she wasn't working, that was—and she'd damn well *have* fun slobbing about and eating her body weight in food meant for Sundays. A fried breakfast, a roast, then sandwiches later, maybe a couple of packets of crisps and a roll of Wine Gums.

The house had been chilly when she'd got up, the nippy air wrapping itself around her wet skin as soon as she'd stepped from the shower. She was snug in her clothes now, and the heating had done a good job of warming the place, even if the pipes creaked and groaned, protesting at the thermostat being turned up.

The breakfast cooked, she ended up shouting from the bottom of the stairs for Damon to come and join her, and his had to be microwaved by the time he'd showered. Funny how they'd both got dressed, forgoing dossing in their pyjamas. They'd been caught out before, being called in to work, and it was just easier to rush out of the house and get there quicker if they didn't have to get ready first.

"This is nice." She leant back in her chair at the kitchen table while Damon munched away. "No one on our fucking earhole."

He nodded, swallowing.

"I nearly switched my phone off." She'd been sorely tempted but had stopped herself at the last minute. She might be a hard-nosed cow, but leaving someone else to do her job, even if it was her day off, didn't sit well.

"Bethany Smith in Shadwell could deal with it if a job comes in," Damon said.

"Not something either her or I would like, you know that. We're both stubborn, both want to solve stuff with our own teams on our own patches. I'm surprised we've got away with our little arrangement so far, you know."

"What, your team not going to Shadwell and helping Bethany out if they get a big case?"

"Hmm."

Tracy had told Bethany that so long as she could handle her city and what went on in it, Tracy would stay away. Like Tracy ever wanted to go there if she could help it. She'd been brought up in Shadwell by an abused mother and a father who liked to bring his friends round to have an illegal fiddle. Little girls were their thing. Years later, one of the men had turned out to be Tracy's chief, but she hadn't recognised him at first. Then she'd killed him, but few people knew that. Best to keep those sorts of shenanigans beneath the stinking rug she'd swept them under.

She shivered. "Fucking hate that place."

"Can't say I'm fond of it. So what are we doing today? Anything?" He placed his knife and fork on his plate then rose to clear up.

She cooked, he cleaned, and vice versa. Rules sorted.

"Nothing. The best pastime, that, bugger all." She stretched her hands upwards, hung her head back, and envisaged the sofa waiting for her to jump on it and relax.

Her work phone rang on the side by the kettle, and she looked at Damon. "You're bloody kidding me. These sodding criminals have no respect. They could at least have waited until tomorrow." Yes, that was an unreasonable thought, but she had about a million of them a day. She didn't reckon she'd be able to stop them flouncing into her head either. It was who she was, a product of her childhood, but her therapist, Sasha Barrows, had helped her come to terms with her peculiarities. Sort of.

Taking Sasha's advice for once, Tracy opted for happiness in her tone rather than anger to deal with this call. It might not be anything major anyway, and she'd have got her knickers all twisted up for no reason. She left the table. Grabbed the phone. Wanted to smash it against the wall.

Anger was winning. So what was new?

She stared at the screen: VIC ATKINS.

Front desk. Lovely. Something had come in then.

She answered. "Yep."

"Sorry to disturb your Sunday, boss…"

You fucking will be. She didn't mean that. *Liar.* "Go on, Vic."

"Body's been discovered at an address in Peacock Lane, number one," he said.

"Not another bloody fire, is it?" It was driving her mental that they hadn't caught the bastard yet.

"Um, no. We're talking murder of a different kind."

"Right. Who's at the scene?"

"James Quinn and Claudia Pringle."

"Who found the body?"

"A Ted Underby."

"So did this Ted just wake up and find the body or what?" That had to sting, going to bed with a live one and getting up in the morning to a dead one.

"No. The victim is a Sara Scott. Ted had gone round there for a bit of an early morning, err, you know."

"We're all adults here, Vic, you can say it. Shag. He'd gone there for a shag. See how easy that was? And?"

Vic coughed. "Well, he got in using the key Sara keeps behind the postbox thing on her outside wall, went into the kitchen to make her a surprise cuppa, then took it up to give it to her. The tea ended up on the carpet."

"Great. Scene contamination. That's just effing fab." It wasn't, it was seriously annoying and would make things a lot harder for SOCO. Come to think of it, there was a new lead officer in that department, and Tracy had yet to meet him. Paul Dunley, something like that. She hadn't really been listening when Chief Winter had told her about him last week.

"SOCO are already there," Vic said. "I've phoned Gilbert."

Tracy loved Gilbert, the elderly ME, but his assistant, that nasty Kathy...she couldn't stand her. They'd known each other since childhood. Funny how relationships soured. But that was all in the past, and Tracy needed to remember that and get on with her job as though there wasn't a mile-wide chasm between her and the woman she'd once called best friend. That saga was a whole other series…

"Okay, me and Damon are on our way." She cut the call, scribbled the address down on a notepad, and handed the page to him. "That's our roast beef up the swanny. The cauliflower cheese I'd planned an' all. From scratch. And shut your mouth. I thought I'd give it a go. How hard can it be to make cheese sauce?"

"No comment." He laughed.

"Oi."

"I gather it's a body." He shoved the last of the breakfast things in the dishwasher then popped in a tablet and set the machine to wash.

"Yeah, some bloke called Ted found her. I'll tell you on the drive over there."

They arrived ten minutes later at Tracy's least favourite estate, the one with the bird names for streets where bad shit always seemed to go down. She parked behind a patrol car and SOCO van opposite the strip of houses

The recent letterbox fires had resulted in the council saying they'd supply CCTV, but you could bet your arse it wouldn't be installed yet. No, that would make Tracy's job too easy. The killer would have been caught on camera if things had been done on time.

She got out of the car and looked around. No cameras on poles or lampposts. Damon pulled protectives out of the boot, and while they suited up, Tracy took in the area. Peacock Lane was a quaint little place—or as quaint as you could get in this part of town at any rate. Just a few thin detached homes in a row, twenty to be exact, a stretch of land opposite which created an edge to a main road, a roundabout close by, both shrouded in faint mist. Frost clung to the grass, helping it to stand tall and proud in its icy grip, and she turned from that to study the houses. Two-up, two-down, she reckoned, the bricks a bit ancient, as though the buildings had gone up just after the Second World War. New front doors and windows, though, which spruced them up a fair bit.

She sighed, zipping up her suit. Gloves on, she said, "Best be getting along then."

"Joy." Damon lifted his hood in place.

Tracy did the same, tucking in her ginger hair, heading across the road. A slim tent had been erected at the front door, and Claudia Pringle stood in front of it. A quick glance to the right showed James Quinn at the farthest house, number twenty, talking to someone on the step, the cosy yellow glow of the hallway light spilling out and illuminating his uniform.

"Where's the man who found her?" Tracy asked.

"Up there in his car." Claudia pointed to a row of them sitting at the kerb. "Red Volvo. It checks out as his, and he's clean, not even a speeding fine or parking ticket. Ted Underby."

"Okay, we'll get him over and done with first."

They went to his car, and Tracy got her ID out and held it up at the driver's window. Ted joined them on the path, closing his door.

"Hi, I'm DI Tracy Collier, and this is DS Damon Hanks. Can you go through what happened?"

He nodded. "I'm seeing her. Sara, I mean. Neither of us want anything permanent, so we go on dates every now and then and, um, get together other times."

"You mean to have sex?" Blunt as.

"Err, yes. She leaves a key wedged behind her postbox, and she said to just use it if I wanted to come round. She has another fella as well as me."

Ooer, Matron. "What happens if you turn up there and she's with someone else?"

"Funny enough, it's never happened."

Strange set of affairs, but whatever floats your tackle. "So you used the key. What time was this?"

"About ten to nine. Thought I'd make her a cuppa and, you know… I opened up, put the key back, then went in, straight to the kitchen. Sorted her tea, went upstairs. Saw her…saw her like that, and rang my brother, right there in the bedroom. He's a copper. Glen Underby. Shadwell. He said to dial nine-nine-nine."

"What did you do after you were put through to us? You know, your *local* station, as opposed to the one *miles* away in the city?" Snipe.

His cheeks flushed. "I came outside like the man on the phone said to. Waited for those coppers to arrive. I told them what had happened, and I was asked to sit in my car. Then you came."

"Where were you prior to this?"

"At home."

"Can anyone vouch for you?"

"My sister. We house share. She was up from two with her nipper. The baby crying woke me up, so I sat with her. We put the telly on and watched a film once the littlun had dropped back off."

"Okay. We'll have to check that, obviously, but for now, you can go home. You okay to drive?"

"Yeah. I've calmed down a bit now."

"An officer can either come round to take a formal statement, or you can visit the station. Up to you, but I want it done later today."

"I'll go down. Take my sister. She can confirm I was with her while we're at it."

"Perfect. Give Damon here your address and phone number in case we need to pop in on you for any reason, then go. Take care now."

She moved away while that was going on, trying to calm her irrational temper. *Fancy ringing your bloody brother.* With Damon finished and Ted driving off, they returned to number one, signed the log with Claudia, and stepped into the tent, which had created a porch. Booties on, they entered the house. Two SOCOs stood in the hallway staring at the floor, and one of them turned at their arrival. His face mask was up, and she didn't recognise his eyes.

Might be that Dunley fella.

"All right, boss," the other one said.

Mr Unfamiliar coughed. "Ah, you must be Tracy Collier. I'm Paul Dunnings, new lead SOCO." He lowered his mask briefly so she could get a gander at him.

She followed suit. "Yes, that's me, and this is my partner, DS Damon Hanks. We won't shake hands. Gloves and whatnot."

"I was just going to say..." Paul snapped his mask back in place.

Ah, did they have someone here who thought he'd joined a team who didn't know protocol? Of course she wouldn't shake hands. Of course she didn't need reminding.

Much. Sometimes you do whatever the hell you like.

Fuck you.

He'd best not knob her off. He'd experience the sharp side of her tongue if he tried it. Kathy was her preferred victim regarding verbal attacks, then Simone York, the drippy PC, but Tracy didn't mind adding a third to the mix. Variety was the spice of life.

"How do you want to play this?" She was being polite. For now. She usually entered a scene and did what she had to do without running it by anyone, and the last SOCO lead had been happy with that, but this one might want to run things differently. She'd have to allow him some leeway. Maybe.

Paul's eyebrows rose as if he hadn't been expecting what she'd said. "Good of you to ask, but I've been briefed on the way it goes on around here, so continue as normal. I'll shout if you do something to piss me off."

"And I'll shout back. Loudly. Might even get my claws out if you're really unlucky. Were you briefed on *that* an' all?" She raised her own eyebrows, putting her mask back over her mouth and nose.

And the bastard laughed. "I was. Oh, we're going to have fun."

The twinkles in his eyes bothered her, as did the seconds-too-long stare that occurred between them. A flirty stare on his part, a murderous one on hers. He'd better have been told she was with Damon more than just at work, otherwise, this Paul would be finding out how hard her knee felt against his groin. His bollocks would end up inside him if he wasn't careful.

He seemed to get the message, and the twinkles died.

"Body?" She cocked her head, all business.

"Upstairs," Paul said.

She didn't thank him, instead going up there, Damon's low chuckle following. On the landing, she waited for him to stand beside her.

"That wasn't my imagination, was it?" she whispered.

"What, him eyeing you up?"

"Yeah, the cheeky git."

"I think he knows where he stands now."

"There's rules about that sort of shit in the workplace. We're a couple, but we don't behave that way on the job. Unprofessional twat."

"There's rules about kicking someone in the nuts, too. I saw your leg twitch."

She smiled, her cheeks bunching beneath the mask. "Let's hope he cottoned on to it as well then. Means he'll keep his distance."

Mr Unfamiliar had switched to *too* familiar for her liking. So she didn't dwell on it, she walked along the landing to the open doorway and stood there surveying the scene.
Gordon Bennett!

CHAPTER THREE

Olivia's toothbrush sat beside Sara's on the worktop. It had taken a while for him to find it, and it had been in her bag. But he had them, and that was the main thing.

Olivia had unsettled Mike, and he didn't like it. At all. Her finishing with him wasn't something he'd thought she'd actually do. She'd hinted at it from time to time in their two months together, during her stints of moaning, but he'd thought she was all mouth and no trousers.

He hadn't wanted another woman to leave him.

The shock that had gone through him upon seeing her up and about this morning, though... He didn't know if he'd get over that. He'd planned to shower, see if he could sort his face after Sara had clawed at him. He'd had to use her electric toothbrush to clean under her nails when he'd finished killing her, then took the brush with him. It sat on his worktop now, almost glaring at him from across the room. Well, he'd show it what he could do if it kept on. He had a waste disposal unit in his sink. He'd rip the damn head off and shove it down there. That'd teach it.

His jitters were worse from the coffee. The comedown from what he'd done, twice in a matter of hours, wasn't as he'd expected, not so early anyway. He thought he'd have been hyper for days like he'd been with *her*, but he just wanted to go to bed. Sleep it off.

Two in such a short space of time wasn't good on the old equilibrium.

Woozy, he got up and wandered over to the fridge. He'd have a sandwich, that'd sort him out. But not jam. No, not that. Then he'd have a kip on the sofa. Afterwards, he'd have to decide where he went from here.

The first dog was his birthday present from Dad, a squiggly little puppy, something to do with the Irish, so his father had just said. Mike didn't care about that. All he knew was the pet was his, just his, and he'd be friends with her forever. At eight, he was old enough to take her for walks and feed her, but Dad assured he'd clean up any mess she made while she was still small. Once she understood she had to do her business outside, things would get easier. Dad was good at explaining, and Mike reckoned he'd remember breakfast at seven, dinner at six.

Her grey fur tickled his nose every time he snuggled his face into it, and he giggled, the happiest he'd been in a long time. Dad looked happy, too, sitting on the living room floor with him, and that was rare these days, the happiness. Mum was good at taking the shine off things, and she'd do that once she got up. For now, though, Mike would play with his new best friend, and later, Dad said they'd teach her how to sit. Tomorrow would be learning 'paw'.

An hour passed on this Saturday morning, and the creak of the floorboards above shouted: She's getting up. Better watch yourself. *Mike's tummy did that funny thing it always did whenever Mum was near, and he swallowed, stroking the puppy to calm himself. That didn't work, so he licked his teeth instead.*

There. That was better.

"All right, son?" Dad asked, seeming nervous himself if him running his hands through his hair

was a big fat clue. It stuck up all over the place. He stood, his arms hanging by his sides.

Dad was blond, and Mike's hair was brown with bits of red in it, like Mum's. He hated having the same hair as her. One day, when he was a man, he'd shave it all off.

"Yeah, I'm fine," Mike lied.

They always did that. Told fibs to each other.

"You let me handle this," Dad said.

Handle what?

Mike didn't feel well. Something bad was going to happen.

Her tromping footsteps coming down the stairs had him feeling worse. The doggy whimpered. Mike had his back to the door, but he knew she *was there, standing in the frame. He imagined her nightie and her smelly dressing gown that needed a good wash. Her hair would have its usual morning cotton wool appearance. He saw her in his mind's eye and tried not to shudder, but it was hard, so hard.*

"What was that noise?" she snapped.

No saying happy birthday. No asking him if he liked his present.

"Not sure what noise you mean, Peggy." One of Dad's hands shook.

"Sounded like an animal," she said.

Mike clutched his pet tighter, and she yelped. I'm sorry.

"What the fuck?" Mum stormed in and rounded Mike, coming to stop in front of him and glaring down. "What. Is. That?" She pointed at Mike's lap.

"It's the lad's present," Dad said. "For his birthday."

"You didn't ask me if he could have a dog." Mum bunched her fists.

"Aren't you going to wish the boy a happy birthday?" Dad glanced across at her.

"I need coffee. I can't handle this. An animal. Of all the things." Mum walked out of sight. "I'm not cleaning up its crap and piss, and if it chews anything, it's gone."

Mike knew what 'gone' meant, but Dad didn't. Mike had to keep that a secret. If he told, Mum would make him gone, too. She'd made his gerbil gone, and the neighbour's cat. He'd watched her, sticking a compass from his maths set into their bodies, and they'd squealed with pain, then she'd...done what she'd done, and they weren't here anymore.

She was a monster, and Mike was afraid of those.

CHAPTER FOUR

Still on the landing, Tracy shook her head, unable to believe what she was seeing. Was this for real or just her mind playing tricks on her? "What the actual eff?" she whispered.

Damon came to stand beside her. "Oh, nasty."

Blood coated the far wall in splashes, blobs, and lines, as though someone had used a paintbrush and flicked it, creating a spatter picture. It stood out against the white background, and Tracy dreaded to look at the body and see what a mess it was—all that blood had to come from somewhere.

A SOCO turned from taking pictures. "You'll not believe how they got hold of that blood. Use the evidence steps, will you? Too much mess on the floor."

Blood had also landed there, and on the blue quilt cover, the pillowcases, and bedside cabinets. Some speckled the ceiling, so the person who'd done this had to have it all over them—or they'd put on protective clothing.

"Somebody got dirty," she said.

"Whoever it was had a shower," the SOCO replied. "Residue in the tray."

"Right." She walked over the steps placed a stride apart and stopped next to the bed.

Sara Scott's brunette hair had been shorn off, placed either side of her head on the pillow—macabre, hairy tongues. It appeared scissors had been used—the killer had enjoyed a good hacking. Her eyebrows were missing, as was the skin beneath, sliced away and placed beneath her nose, a long, disjointed moustache that must have stuck solid to her face by now. Her earlobes had been removed and rested on her open eyes in place of irises.

Someone was angry.

Someone had so much rage in them they probably couldn't think straight.

Sara was naked, her neck showing signs of strangulation. Her torso had tiny holes in it, wider than a pin, closer in size to a Bic pen nib. Tracy would have thought Bethany Smith in Shadwell hadn't caught the right killer in the Tic Tac Toe case if it wasn't for numbers beside each dot, a Sharpie or the like used to write them, black ink. Eyes had been drawn, cartoonish, and a downturned mouth.

"Dot to dot," she said. "I'll take a photo of that, because you can bet it'll create a picture. There wouldn't be eyes and a gob otherwise." She took her phone out and snapped a few. Studied the pattern to see if she could work out what it would be. But there were too many holes and numbers. "I'll get Nada in to help. She can sit and draw this." She tapped out a message, apologising for asking her to do work-related things on a Sunday, then sent the photo.

Tracy: I COULD DO WITH YOU COMING IN TO WORK, TO BE HONEST. WE NEED CCTV, NEXT OF KIN, SOCIAL MEDIA, AND A BACKGROUND CHECK DOING. SARA SCOTT, ONE PEACOCK LANE.

Nada: ON MY WAY.

Tracy: CHEERS.

Nada: OH, BLIMEY. JUST SEEN THE IMAGE. WHAT THE HELL?

Tracy: YOU SHOULD SEE THE REST OF HER.

Nada: SHIT.

Tracy put her phone away and sighed. Shit was right. Whoever had done this had a score to settle, immense rage directed at the victim. What on earth had she done to deserve this? She had to be pretty nasty to elicit this kind of reaction. There was killing, then there was going overboard.

"What a fucking nutter," she said.

"Yep." Damon was still on the landing.

"I'll explain in case you can't see properly. There's a large plastic bowl," she said, "the kind you use for mixing cakes in. Her arm's balanced on top, and the inside of her arm has been slit downwards. The blood drained into it. There's still a bit left in the bottom, but I bet they used this to splatter the walls." The question was: How had Sara been kept still enough to stop her flailing around while the blood poured? Had she been sat on? Knocked unconscious? "There's less than a body's worth of blood in this room and the bowl." She turned to the SOCO. "Thoughts?"

"They probably let the amount out that they wanted, then killed her. Heart stops pumping, so does the blood. It'd still seep until coagulation, but not to the degree it had when she was alive."

"Hmm. What's your take on this, Damon?"

"I was going to say the same thing—unless it's gone on and through the mattress?"

"It has, but not a flood. More like patches where it possibly sloshed out while they were using it to decorate the wall." She swallowed. "And it stinks in here. Manky meat."

"Dried blood," the SOCO said.

I know, divvo. I was just saying. "Yes, quite..." She glanced at Damon.

He lifted his eyebrows, probably warning her not to say something catty. "Come out so I can have a look?"

She nodded and plodded over the steps. "Mind the *dried blood* smell. It isn't manky meat like I thought. Silly me."

"Pack it in," Damon muttered and entered. Beside the bed, he leant over. "Earlobes on eyeballs? And I get what you mean about the holes in the stomach. This setup had to have taken a lot of time. Couple of hours?"

"Yes, to prod all those holes and work out whether your image is going to come out right would take a while." Her phone bleeped with a message. She took it out and accessed it. A picture from Nada. She'd obviously printed the original, joined the dots, then snapped a shot of it. "Um, Nada's got back to me."

"And?" Damon stood upright.

"It's an octopus."

"A what?"

"You heard me." She replied to Nada, saying thanks. "So that's a nice clue we're never going to fathom. Mollusc. Eight arms. Massive head. Sea creature. Yep, we've got our work cut out for us. Nice."

Damon came back out. Had a peek. "It's the sort you get in those books. I had them as a kid. Then you colour it in after."

"Well, the only colour that one's got is red." She'd never had a dot-to-dot book, not that she could recall anyway. If she had, she'd pushed the memory into her mind box. Her childhood hadn't been the type for normal things like that.

Voices chattered downstairs.

"Hello!" Gilbert called.

Hopefully he hadn't brought Kathy with him. Gilbert had confessed once that he didn't like her, preferred working on his own, but depending on the severity of the cases, she tagged along. Most of the time these days, though, he sent her out to smaller jobs so he could do autopsies and scene visits in peace, or vice versa.

"Up here!" Tracy peered over the banister.

"Ah, my dear, you're here," he said. "I thought I saw your car out there."

She squinted to make out whether Kathy was there. Unfortunately, she was.

"It's a weird one for you," Tracy said.

"On my way."

She faced Damon. Whispered, "Shitbag is here, too."

"Don't bite. You know how you're meant to deal with her now. Professionally. She means nothing to you—or that's how you need to behave anyway."

Kathy could never mean nothing. When they'd been much younger, Tracy had told her things about her life while she'd been drunk. She'd believed the next day, because Kathy hadn't mentioned it, that her so-called friend had forgotten. Turned out, years later, Kathy had chosen to remain quiet about it, all the while berating Tracy for how she acted, how snide she was with people. Kathy was fully aware of the reasons, yet she'd played a cruel game, letting Tracy believe she was a bitch, when really, her behaviour was a product of what she'd endured.

Now it was Tracy's job not to allow herself to fall back on that as an excuse. She'd been raised badly, had been through awful things, but that was no reason to treat people like shit. However, old habits were hard to break, and being kind to Kathy wasn't ever going to be on the agenda. Tracy was much better than she used to be with people, though, so progress in trying to change herself had been made.

She moved to stand beside Damon on the right-hand side of the door so there was no chance of Kathy 'accidentally' brushing past her, giving her an elbow nudge or whatever. Gilbert came up the stairs first, widening his eyes as a signal to warn Tracy of what she already knew: *She's with me.* Tracy nodded slightly, then Kathy herself appeared, *her* eyes the complete opposite, narrowed and spiteful over her face mask.

You'll never beat me in being Queen Bitch, missus, so don't even try.

Gilbert stopped at the doorway, Kathy almost bumping into him she was that intent on glaring at Tracy and not watching where she was going.

"What a thing to be called out for on a Sunday," Gilbert said. "Still, it saved me eating too much and partaking in a few gins this afternoon. My waistline will thank me, not to mention my gallbladder. Bloody thing's playing up. Got a few stones. Too small to deal with at present."

"Sorry to hear that," Tracy said.

"But there's others worse off." He shook his head. "Like that poor lady there."

"We've been in," Tracy said. "I'll tell you now, the image on the stomach is of an octopus. If you've got an insight into that, be my guest and share it."

"Someone with lots of arms in different areas," Kathy said, as if it were fact.

Tracy ignored her. It was for the best. Just being in her company was enough to set her teeth on edge. She'd had a really massive go at her once, and it had been totally wrong of her to have done so. She'd risked losing her job by talking to her the way she had, but at the time, getting the words out had been more important. Saying her piece so she could move on had taken priority. Real life had encroached on work, old hurts surfacing. If she had to do it all again, she would—she'd slayed a lot of demons that day.

Gilbert waved at the SOCO in the room. "Okay to put down a few more steps?" He pointed to a stack by the door. "My assistant is with me."

"Yep, two secs." The SOCO, who'd switched from taking pictures to measuring blood arcs, came over and placed some down, leading to the other side of the bed. "There you go." He returned to the wall and got back to work.

"Thank you."

Gilbert went to the right, Kathy to the left. He popped his bag on a spare step and stood perusing the body.

"What a strange sight," he said. "Who on earth would want to do this?" He blinked several times. "Oh. That blood in the bowl. That isn't nice at all."

"We had a chat about that, theorising what went on there," Tracy said. "I said there wasn't enough blood in the room for it to be all she had in her."

"Quite right," Gilbert said. "While this room is liberally decorated with it, considering the majority of bodies have a few pints, this isn't all of it. That chap downstairs, Paul, he said it was okay for me to touch." He reached out and lifted her hand. "Okay, no rigor as yet, but it's on the way. She's a tiny bit stiff." With her temperature taken, he paused for a moment. "Hmm. Between three and four a.m."

"Give or take?" Kathy asked.

"Uh, no. I'd have said if it was. Definitely between those times." He cleared his throat. "If you look at one of the longer bloodstains on the sheet, it would appear her arm rested there. Perhaps when the killer went Van Gogh?"

"More like Jackson Pollock," Kathy said.

Why didn't she just shut the hell up? Why did she have to correct everyone all the damn time? Tracy had already acknowledged she saw herself in Kathy, but when Kathy did it, it seemed wrong. Sasha Burrows had mentioned some people had that attitude: *All right for me to do it but not for you.* Okay, so Tracy was one of those people.

Now shut up yourself.

"Back to discussing the body and not artists," Tracy said. "So her arm was then posed over the bowl afterwards, as if the killer wanted us to know how they caught the blood. The bowl says it all, we didn't need it spelling out."

"Some people aren't as clever as you, Miss Know-It-All," Kathy muttered.

Oh. So she wanted to start, did she?

Don't bite. "Are you one of the thickos then?" *Too late. The words are out.* "Wouldn't you have got that?"

A tic beside Kathy's eye twitched. "Back to the body and not sniping…"

"You started it, woman. Don't expect no comeback when you're snarking." She waited for a response. None. *Round one of the day to me.* "Gilbert, is there anything else you've picked up on?"

"Strangulation. Earlobes cut off after death, quite some time after, up to half an hour, possibly the time it took for the blood to be spattered. Minimal blood on the ears. Probably lopped off with extremely sharp scissors."

"At odds with her hair. That's been chopped at."

He bent over. "Yes, probably a knife. The cut ends aren't a nice clean snip. A bizarre thing to do, leaving her shorn like this."

"The hair's probably significant." Kathy.

You think? "That's why it was removed." *And since when were you a bloody detective, Kathy?* "Okay, we need to get going." Translated to: *I don't want to be near you any longer.* "See you, Gilbert."

She turned and walked down the stairs in search of Paul, glancing over her shoulder to ensure Damon was with her. He was right there, thank God. She didn't fancy a strange staring match with the lead SOCO again. He was in the kitchen, head cocked while contemplating a pair of scissors on the draining board.

"Ah, had your fill, have you?" he asked.

"Enough for the moment, yes. Are those the scissors used on the victim?"

"Seems so."

"For the ears."

"I'd say yes. There's a knife in the washing-up bowl. It has a hair on it. Long, same colour as the victim's."

"So he hasn't stuck to just the bedroom. He's spread himself out a bit."

"Oh yes. You might want to go in the living room as well," Paul said. "I heard you don't like doing walkarounds with the likes of me breathing down your neck, so off you go and see for yourself."

Sounded like he was giving her permission, the cheeky sod.

She stopped the budding retort and the flounce, willing herself to behave like a normal human. "Okay. Doesn't sound good."

"It'd spoil the surprise if I gave you fair warning." He bagged the scissors.

She turned and strutted out and down the hallway. At the living room door, she took a breath and readied herself for the worst. Then she stepped inside. The room spanned the width of the house. Ahead, a set of French doors to the left, a bay window to the right. On the adjacent wall to the doors, a fireplace with a TV mounted on the wall. A U-shaped cream sofa filled the opposite end, a large fluffy black rug in the centre over grey laminate. Spotless, apart from the things on the sofa. She dodged a SOCO who was on hands and knees searching the rug fibres. Stared down at the items, which had been placed on each of the six wide seats.

A dot-to-dot book, open, a page ripped out. She'd bet it'd been one of an octopus. A wooden dolly clothes peg, the word BITCH written on the side. Next came a picture of a dog, probably cut from a magazine, the paper glossy. She shifted her gaze along to an empty packet of crisps—Space Raiders, pickled onion. Then came a few scattered grains of uncooked rice, and lastly, what appeared to be a liver.

She glanced at Damon. "I have nothing."

He moved closer and inspected everything. "Um, this is too obscure. They mean nothing to us but probably everything to the killer. These clues aren't going to tell us bugger all until they're explained to us—if we catch them and if they choose to speak about it."

"Okay, let's have a bash at talking it out. The dot-to-dot book—from childhood? The clothes peg—a woman who is thought of as a bitch uses them? The dog—they owned one or still do; or maybe the bitch owns it? The crisps and rice, some kind of memory, but the liver? You're right. We have nothing. We're better off going back to the station and working from there after we've spoken to Quinn. He might have got something from the neighbours."

But in all honesty, she had to get out of the house. It was all too weird for words.

CHAPTER FIVE

*M*ike had received a book from Nanny. Dot to dot, as always. She'd popped round to wish him a happy birthday but hadn't stayed long. Mum had remained in the kitchen, smoking her fags.

Dad had hugged Nanny and whispered, "Thanks for coming. I know how much you can't stand her."

Nanny didn't like Mum at all, and that made two of them. Three, if you counted Dad, but sometimes he acted as though he reckoned she was okay. Mike didn't understand it, Dad swinging from liking to hating—and he did hate, he'd muttered that once. Mike also swung from like to hate, and he didn't understand himself either.

Mum wasn't a nice person, even though she made a good show sometimes of pretending to be one. That was when her friends came round, and she had a lot of those. Most were as bitchy as her, but there was one, Gabby Raines, who told Mum to stop being horrible to Mike, that he was only a little lad and didn't deserve the way she spoke to him.

Mike loved Gabby.

Nanny had left after a quick cup of tea, cuddling Mike to her squishy body. He wished he could live with her—she'd offered that once or twice—but that would mean leaving Dad with Mum, and Mike needed to be here for when Dad was upset.

He joined the dots on the first picture, and it created an octopus, with funny wide eyes and a smiling mouth. The wiggly arms stretched all around, and he reached out for his colouring pencils. He'd use blue for the sea and red for the octopus. The puppy was asleep beside him, pressed close to his leg. He hadn't picked a name for her yet and tried to think of a good one. Right this minute, with his book and his dog, Mum upstairs putting her makeup on and Dad out in the garden tending to the veg patch, Mike was the happiest he'd been in a long time. Well, apart from getting the puppy as a present.

He stared at the octopus, then at the dog.

"Dot," he said. "That's what you're called."

The back door groaned, the sound streaking through into the living room, so Dad must have come inside. The dull thud of vegetables being dropped on the worktop followed, and Dad muttered, "That lot'll go well with the liver."

Mike hated liver, it tasted funny, but Mum said it was good for you, although she never ate it. Said it didn't agree with her. Still, maybe he could eat the sweets Nanny had brought afterwards, and that'd make it all better.

Dad poked his head around the door, and Mike jumped. Seemed he was always jumpy.

"I'm nipping out for a bit," Dad said.

Mike nodded, stroking Dot, uncomfortable with being left in the house with Mum. He'd keep really quiet. She wouldn't hurt him then. "Okay."

"Good lad."

The click of the front door shutting meant Mike's stomach cramped. Dot whimpered. The moan of the landing floorboards gave rise to him feeling sick, and to keep himself occupied, he drew a downturned mouth on the octopus, a creature as sad as he was now. And Dot, she looked sad, too. She got up, tail between her legs, and piddled on the carpet. Mike stared at the wet patch, the book shaking in his hands, the pages whispering: She's coming, she'll see that, and you'll be in trouble.

One footstep on the stairs. Two. Three.

Dot ran to hide beside the chair. She must be afraid of Mum, too. Mike returned his attention to the wee.

53

Four footsteps. Five, six, seven, eight...

He scrabbled to sit on the mess, facing the door. It seeped through his trousers, going cold on his skin, and he shivered from that and the fright winging its way through him. Dot stopped crying, and he was glad about that. Mum would hurt her, make her gone if she made a racket.

Nine, ten...

He held his breath.

Eleven, twelve, and then there she was, standing in the doorway, hands on hips, her face pretty to anyone but Mike and Nanny, her makeup flawless.

"Where's the scutty hound?" she said, glancing about for her.

"Down there, asleep." Mike pointed a wavering finger at the chair.

"Good. See she stays that way an' all. Get in the kitchen. I need help with the veg. It's your favourite tonight. Liver. All special for your birthday. Seven, are you?" She narrowed her eyes.

"Eight." He stood, conscious of the damp patch on his bum.

"Like I'd forget. I was playing with you. Eight years ago today, you wrecked my life. Still haven't been able to lose the weight from it. That's nothing to celebrate, is it?"

He didn't know how he'd wrecked it, but if she said he had, he must have done. She walked away, and he followed, his wet underpants sticking to him. She stood at the worktop, staring at the vegetables Dad had pulled. Onions, potatoes, and a cabbage.

"You can chop the onions," she said without looking at him. "I don't want to fuck up my mascara.

I'm going out tonight with Gabby." She paused. *"To see what's on offer."*

There were so many things she came out with that he didn't understand, but he'd learnt not to question them. She said what she said, no explanation, and he kept it inside, somehow knowing it wouldn't be a good idea to ask Dad. Besides, Mike didn't want to be 'gone', so it was best he kept things to himself.

She whizzed round to watch him as he walked to get a knife from the drawer. "Have you pissed yourself?"

Mike jolted. It was on the tip of his tongue to say no, but then Dot would get poked with the compass, and she'd cry and wonder why Mum was being so cruel.

"Yes," he said. "I'm sorry."

He said that a lot around Mum.

"You will be, I'll make sure of that, and you won't know when the punishment's coming either." She glared at him. *"Now get upstairs and wash. Change your trousers. Hang on. Where did you do it, on the carpet?"*

He nodded.

"Little bastard. You can clean that first. And take your time so the piss itches your skin while it dries."

He grabbed the scrubbing brush and carpet spray out of the cupboard under the sink, glad to get away from her. Didn't even care about the itching so long as he wasn't near that woman. Dot came over, and while he circled the brush over the stain, she licked his hand.

That made it all better.

As did running his tongue over his teeth.

Mike had been watching a programme lately called *Can't Pay, We'll Take it Away*. It had given him the idea, a while back, to buy a uniform, a stab vest, and download a logo that looked similar to those on a High Court writ. At first, the show had brought back painful memories of when the bailiffs had come round because of something Mum had done after she'd found that something 'on offer' and run off with him to start a new life without them. Then they'd been evicted because Dad didn't earn enough on his own to keep up with the high rent. Nanny couldn't help, she wasn't rich—"I'm sorry, I don't have a pot to piss in, son..."—and that meant they'd lived with Nanny then, so Dad could save a deposit for a new, less expensive place, which turned out to be a little flat.

Mike had never been happier there. Until Mum had shown up on the doorstep.

He shoved the memory of *that* out of his head.

He wrenched himself from the past.

For six months, he'd been watching brunette women with red tints in their hair to ensure they lived alone. Recently, two of them had got a boyfriend, but that still left four besides Sara and Olivia. Three were confident types, but one, Anne Walton her name was, seemed a bit slow on the uptake. He'd planned to knock on her door and give her exactly what Mum should have got—a fright from the bailiffs.

He'd found out Anne's name from listening with his car window down while she'd spoken to a neighbour over the fence between their gardens.

"Well," the neighbour had said, "I think you're brave to be by yourself after such a traumatic relationship. Aren't you afraid of him finding you through his friends, though?"

"No, Val," Anne said. "I'm on the other side of town now, and anyway, while he's in prison, I can relax a bit more. I get most of my shopping online so I don't have to go out—you must have seen all the delivery vans."

"Not if I'm at work, I don't." Val had sighed. "PTSD, though." She'd shaken her head. "To have it to such a degree that you can't work... He must have done a right old number on you."

"I'll talk about it all one day, I promise, just not yet." Anne had smiled.

Over the next few weeks, Mike had caught Anne and Val nattering on several occasions, enough for him to build up a profile: Anne Walton, domestic violence survivor, skittish, rarely went out. Hiding from a man named Joseph Vord, who had a rep for being clever with his fists in pubs if anyone got on his nerves. He'd used those fists on Anne, too, had spent a year in the nick for assaulting her, and wasn't due out for two months. She'd lived with Joseph for three years, and he owed money all over the place. The neighbour, Val, was away during the day, annoyed she always worked on a Sunday.

And that was all Mike needed: Sunday, that push to give Anne a visit and what she had coming to her. She'd be Peggy in his head, that bloody mother of his, and she needed teaching a lesson.

He popped his uniform on and looked at himself in the mirror. Yep, he appeared just the same as those men on TV. The only difference was he'd be turning up alone, without a colleague. Maybe Anne wouldn't know enforcement agents didn't work by themselves—or on a Sunday. They always had a partner in case the people they visited got nasty. If she queried that, he'd blag it. Same with the day of the week. He'd add an addition to his fake writ saying the court had permitted a Sunday visit.

With his pouch strapped to his belt, he sorted his writ on the computer and printed it out. Satisfied it appeared authentic enough and contained legal jargon that would flummox the woman into skimming it, he put a long woollen coat over his uniform so his neighbours didn't wonder about the outfit, collected the other things he needed, and set off in his work van, a small white one that no one usually took any notice of. That was the way with them, wasn't it. There were so many on the roads they became invisible.

Outside Anne's house, he slapped on a cap with a wig attached and pressed a sticky-backed moustache in place. He shivered. Peggy used to have a faint one, but the more he'd stared at it, the more prominent it had seemed. She'd dyed it with bleach cream sometimes, but it had still been there, and she hated it. At one point, she'd shaved it off, but it had grown back thicker, wiry.

As ready as he'd ever be, he took his coat off, got out of the van, and walked up Anne's path, the writ in hand. He rang the bell and waited. The net curtain to his right twitched—Anne nosing out, most likely, checking whether Joseph Vord had got out of prison early and was paying her a visit. Mike didn't look that way, just stared ahead until her shadowy figure appeared behind the glass.

The door opened three inches, a gold chain in place, and she peered through at him, eyes wide. "Yes?"

"Anne Walton?"

"Yes?"

"I have a writ from the High Court. You need to settle a debt to the sum of two thousand and fifteen pounds. I'll have to take payment and, failing that, I will remove goods to be sold at auction to cover that debt. Do you have the means to pay this today?"

"What?" She blinked, obviously stunned.

He gritted his teeth for a moment. "Do you have the money, Miss Walton?"

She shook her head, hair swishing. "No! What's it even for?"

"The client is owed monies for a loan taken out by yourself and a Mr Joseph Vord."

Anne gasped and raised her hand to her chin, fingertips fluttering there. "Joseph? I didn't take any loans out with him."

He rocked on his heels. "You must have done. It's been to court, and as he's in prison, he couldn't attend, but you should have done. It's not wise to ignore a court summons. If you'd been there to plead your case, the client may not have applied to the High Court."

"I didn't get any letter telling me to go. I have no idea what you're even talking about."

Mike laughed. "If you knew how many people said that to me every day… If I got a pound for each time I heard it, I'd be a millionaire. Rolling in it."

"I'm not lying, you know." She looked up. "Oh. Would the letter have gone to my former address, do you think? God, this is the first I've heard of this."

"And that. They say those words a lot as well." He fixed her with a mean glare. "I'll ask you one more time. Do you have the funds to settle this debt, Miss Walton?"

"No. I'm on benefits. I can't work at the moment. If it's been to court, surely they'd have allowed some sort of payment plan."

"They did, but because you didn't show, the client applied to the High Court to get payment in full. This is the legal paperwork supporting that." He waggled the fake writ. "Would you like to read it?"

She nodded, tears spilling, her cheeks paling.

He turned it so it faced her. "As you can see, it's all above board." He'd even downloaded a court seal to resemble a genuine letterhead. "Failure to settle means I'll come in and take an inventory of goods. If you can't pay, I'll take it away." God, he nearly laughed at using the programme title. But he wasn't here to joke about. This was serious. He schooled himself calm.

"Can I contest this?" she asked. "Joseph must have faked my signature when he applied for the loan. There's got to be some way this can be resolved if I've had nothing to do with it. You can't expect me to pay when there's no proof I even signed the application."

"No, the time for that is past. High Court writs are the end of the line. You'll have to deal with it afterwards."

"I have *no* money. Literally none. The next time I get some is at the end of the month, and it's barely enough to live on, so how I can pay a debt that isn't mine, I don't know."

She was getting on his nerves, being feisty. He hadn't expected her to have any fire in her belly. Anne hadn't displayed any signs of fighting her corner when she'd been chatting to Val. And speaking of Val... He needed to get a move on before she came home.

He placed a foot in the gap between the door and the frame. "Then I'm coming in."

"But you can't do that!"

"You'll find I can. Paragraph three." He held the writ closer.

"Oh God..."

"If you don't let me in willingly, I'll have to break the chain, but I *will* come in." He sounded just like that fella on the telly. Mike had memorised all their lines. He folded the writ and slid it beneath his stab vest.

She drew the chain across, opened the door wider, and stepped back.

And her hair, it was just like Peggy's.

Rage mounted, growing too strong, so Mike reined it in. He didn't need it just yet. He walked inside and closed the door. "I'll just have a look around and list your possessions. If you could follow me, please. I have a body cam on"—he pointed to the plastic pretend one on his vest pocket—"but we still prefer people to watch what we're doing. Likewise, we have to watch what *you're* doing. We can't have you off in another room hiding goods. They belong to the court now, and if you try to keep any of them, you're effectively stealing."

"Stealing my own things? But that's ridiculous."

"Ridiculous is not paying the money you owe, Miss Walton. Ridiculous is having me turn up. If you and Mr Vord had continued with the loan repayments, none of this would be happening."

She shook from head to foot. "But I *didn't take out the loan!*"

Of course she hadn't, but that was neither here nor there. Dad hadn't taken a loan out in the past either, and no one had cared about that. For the purposes of his plan, Anne had behaved just like Mum, who'd forged Dad's signature after she'd left them to be with that other man. With Mum unable to pay, they'd sent bailiffs.

They'd eaten a lot of beans on toast during that time.

"You've got to be a certain type of person to do this job," Anne shrieked.

Mike didn't like her raising her voice that way. It was rude.

So he punched her in the face.

She staggered back, aiming for the corner, where she turned to face it, wedging herself in and covering her head with her forearms. Probably from practise when Joseph had beaten the shit out of her. She'd gone straight into survival mode, all her previous courage deserting her. She whimpered, shuddering, and he imagined her as Mum, cowering, afraid of him. He was going to do to Mum what he'd always wanted, and while he'd already assuaged some of that need again with Sara and Olivia, the desire to continually obliterate Peggy Redmond seared strong. It overtook him in a great wave, flooding his system.

He didn't have time to do to Anne what he'd done with Sara—the blood spatter—nor for what he'd done with Olivia, but he could leave his mark good and proper, so when the police found her, they'd know it was him. Those clues, they said so much about Mike, representing the years of hell he'd spent in a childhood he shouldn't have endured. If only Dad had never met Mum. But then Mike wouldn't exist.

Maybe that wouldn't be such a bad thing. He wouldn't have to suffer then, would he, then and now.

Mike walked forward, hands out, and he grabbed her hair, spinning her to face him. He pressed her back into the corner then fitted his gloved hands around her neck, and she had her eyes closed, as if she needed to shut him out, the sight of him, what he was doing. Had her mind shorted and she imagined he was Joseph? Were they both seeing people other than who they really were? And why wasn't she screaming? Was that a result of the PTSD Val had mentioned?

"Open your fucking eyes, Peggy."

She did, wide, her mouth skewing to one side.

"You made us lose our home," he said. "While you were off opening your legs with that man, we had to live with Nanny. You need to suffer for what you did, for making Dad cry with worry."

Peggy didn't answer, and her lashes fluttered, as though she struggled with looking at him and she wanted to shut her eyes again.

"What have you got to say for yourself, you bitch?"

A whimper. Good, that meant she was afraid.

"Answer me," he snarled, the red mist getting thicker.

"I don't know who Peggy is." She could barely get the words out, and they sounded hoarse, garbled. "I'm Anne. Take my things and get out. Please, please, just get out."

"You can't tell me what to do anymore, woman. You're nothing. A worthless piece of shit."

She flinched as though those words brought back memories. Maybe Joseph had said them to her. Maybe, once upon a time, she'd believed them to be true.

Mike tightened his grip, pleased at her cheeks going red. "I'm going to kill you over and over for the rest of my life."

He clamped with more force, the sound of her choking music to ears that had been starved of a mother's kind words—words he'd longed to hear. Peggy still refused to say them even now in this room, that he was a good boy, that she loved him, and she'd never been prouder of anyone in her life. That she was sorry for making all the Dots gone.

His hands shook from the strength he needed to strangle her, and he ground his teeth. She lowered her arms from the top of her head to grip his wrists, tried to push him away, digging her nails into his skin just above the gloves, but he was stronger than her, with a will of iron to see this through, and she was losing this game fast.

Once the light faded from her eyes and her hands dropped to her sides, he let her go, his biceps spasming. She thudded to the floor in a slump, and he stared at her for a short while, taking in the fact that Peggy was gone. He left her there to go upstairs and collect her toothbrush. It wasn't electric like Sara's, but he put stripy toothpaste on the pink plastic one just the same, returning to the living room to scrub at her nails and fingertips. He used a cloth from the kitchen to wipe away the paste, then stuffed both in his pouch, little souvenirs from a productive trip.

He withdrew the compass he'd stabbed Sara and Olivia with and placed it on the arm of the sofa. Kicked Peggy, following the insistent urge to do so, the one he'd often contemplated obeying as a kid. He dragged her flat to the floor and posed her, legs wide open like Peggy had done for that man, then he undid her pink blouse and pushed the fronts aside.

He went back outside, checking for anyone watching. At the van, he collected his other bag and, in the house again, placed it on the floor. He took out the page from the book of dots and rested it on her stomach as a template, using the compass to press through the dots until all of them had been done. Blood stained the paper. He put it on the floor beside her and used his Sharpie to write the numbers on her skin, then screwed the image up and threw it in his bag. He drew the appropriate things that couldn't be revealed by joining the dots, running his tongue over his teeth to keep him calm. He had to hurry. That Val woman would be back soon. She worked at Sainsbury's from ten until two. Maybe he'd go in there next week to buy his lunch, get served by her on the till. See if she had red eyes from crying about Peggy being gone.

He cut Mum's hair off with his super-sharpened cheese knife, placing the strands on the floor, then, just because he could, he held the snake-tongue end of the blade beneath her nose and contemplated shoving the forks up either side of her septum. How many times had he gripped this knife as a child and thought about doing that very thing?

No. Don't.

Instead, he sliced her eyebrows off—a bit messy because of the blood seeping—and put them above her top lip. He spied a sewing basket beside the sofa and grabbed the scissors there, snipping her earlobes off and balancing them on her bulging eyes. Blood from them dribbled off and down, red tears streaking across her temples.

She was as complete as he could get her, so he got up and put the scissors on the draining board in the kitchen, just so. Back with Peggy's body, he placed his items on her sofa—only three this time—packed his things up, checked he hadn't left anything behind he shouldn't have, and ran upstairs to do something in the bathroom. Then he left her house, keeping the door ajar. Val could find her despicable friend. She'd soon realise Peggy deserved everything she'd got from Mike and Joseph.

He drove away, no CCTV on his journey—he'd checked while in the planning stage—and removed his moustache and cap wig once he'd arrived at his house. Absolutely knackered, the spending of rage for the third time in a few hours sending him weak, he entered his place on what felt like hollow legs. With his uniform and gloves in the washing machine being jostled around with an Ariel liquid pod, he put her toothbrush in Nanny's old biscuit tin along with Sara's and Olivia's. Couldn't stand them looking at him.

The bloodied paper with the dot image on it belonged elsewhere. He flattened it out and displayed it with the other two, inside its own frame on the living room wall. He'd soon have loads of them, something to remind him of how many times he'd killed Peggy. Compass and knife soaking in bleach in the washing-up bowl, he went and had a bath.

It was his due after all that hard work.

Clean and snuggly in his fleece pyjamas, Mike took a breather and created the peg dolls for Olivia and Anne. Sara's leant against the wall on the mantel in her garish outfit, the material from

Peggy's skirt, the one he hated the most. He'd made that dolly in his car after he'd arrived home from killing her. Now, he concentrated on creating two replicas.

He smiled. They'd look pretty together, all in a row.

CHAPTER SIX

For a quick breather before they visited Sara's next of kin, Tracy sat in the incident room sipping a lovely hot coffee from the machine she'd bought for her team. They needed a decent drink; the vending machine stuff was awful.

Damon was on his computer helping Nada out, doing searches regarding the victim's past, while

Nada had finished with CCTV, which had thrown up nothing, and now she trawled social media sites. Together they'd patch together a life story of sorts. Tracy had printed out a picture of Sara, taken from Facebook, and stuck it on one of the whiteboards.

She stood and went over to it. "Okay, let's get some info down under this." She tapped the photo. "Then we need to set off and see the parents, the poor sods."

There had been a delay on that. Mr and Mrs Scott had landed at Doncaster Sheffield Airport, formerly known as Robin Hood, earlier today after a package holiday in Malta. Nada had phoned them while they'd waited for their luggage, not telling them what it was about, and they'd said their arrival at home would be in an hour or two.

Damon called out, "Sara Scott. Address: one Peacock Lane. Age: twenty-nine. Place of employment: Nichols and Merchant, an advertising firm. Vehicle: A white Kia. Parents: Benjamin and Ivory, thirty-eight Goose Close. Siblings: None." He paused for Tracy to catch up with writing then gave the registration number of the car.

"Thanks. Nada?" Tracy said.

"It appears that along with Ted Underby, Sara may have been seeing a Jacob Mannings. Lots of innuendo on Facebook posts, flirting, and generally both of them cropping up on the same comment threads."

"Ted mentioned he and her weren't exclusive." Tracy wrote that down.

"Sara had three hundred and seventeen friends, and only fifteen of them tended to crop up regularly on her posts. They live here. I've made a list and will do a search on all, then give them a ring while you're with the parents, okay?"

"Yep. If any seem dodgy, let me know and we'll give them a visit." Tracy found a face-to-face meeting yielded more via expressions and body language, but with fifteen of the buggers to speak to, that would take some time. "Actually, when we've gone, call the rest of the team. They can go and see these people. They'll only need to clock on for about three hours."

Lara, Erica, Alastair, and Tim would make things easier instead of Tracy, Damon, and Nada struggling as a three-person unit.

"What else have you found?" she asked.

"She's on Facebook and Instagram," Nada said. "She also contributes to posts on Nichols and Merchant's Fb page—she's good at communicating with the public who're asking questions. Nothing sinister going on. No arguments, no sniping from commenters on her own wall."

"What about Ted Underby, the fella who found her? Is he there?"

"I haven't got to him yet on his own social media, but he doesn't comment much on Sara's. He's not one of the fifteen regulars."

"As you know, we've spoken to him anyway," Tracy said. "His brother's a copper in Shadwell."

"Doesn't mean he isn't a weirdo," Nada said.

"True. He didn't strike me as one, though, and he has an alibi. He was with his sister and her nipper, but that could be a lie and she's the sort who's willing to cover for him, but for now, I'm not bothered about him." She looked at Damon. "Anything interesting from her past?"

"Nope, just the usual. Birth, schooling, college, work. No priors." He got up to take the marker off her and write the info up.

She returned to the desk where her coffee was and drank it while thinking for a bit. "I need a list of her work colleagues. We'll get them visited as well—tomorrow will do. Right, we'd better go and deliver the news." She sighed.

In the car, she headed for the bird-name estate. "So, let's think about what Quinn told us. No neighbours saw anything, which isn't surprising, given that it was the middle of the night when her murder happened, but one heard a car turn up. The resident doesn't know what time that was—they have no alarm clock and didn't bother checking on their phone. Can't say I blame them. I'd just try to get back to sleep, too. But it's something—the killer used a vehicle, so it probably wasn't anyone in Sara's street, otherwise, they'd have just walked to hers, done the deed, then went home again. It's just a shame CCTV had nothing, but that's information in itself an' all. Either that was a lucky break, they didn't care if they got seen, or they know where the cameras are. If that's the case, we're talking planning, a person who's meticulous and doesn't intend getting caught."

"I'd say the latter. Who the hell wants to get caught?" Damon said. "Then again, some do it for just that reason."

"Exactly. Now, I'm going to say this is someone who was familiar with her. Got to be if they knew where she kept her key—so it could be a past boyfriend."

"Or conversely, someone who's watched her and spotted either Ted or that Jacob fella—if he's even been seeing her—going inside her house."

She drove along the main road opposite Sara's. SOCOs were still there, but Gilbert's car had gone. Claudia Pringle stood outside the front door tent, looking cold and grumpy. At least she'd put on a hi-vis jacket and gloves since they'd last seen her.

"She's going to freeze her tits off by the end of her shift." Tracy took a left off the roundabout.

"I don't miss those days," Damon said.

"Me neither."

'Those days' had been full of Tracy pretending her childhood hadn't happened. She'd coasted through her life on the beat desperately trying to be someone else—a woman who wasn't tainted and fucked up. It had worked for a while, but snippets of her past had crept in, and to stop herself from getting hurt by them, she'd become a bitter and twisted bitch who was angry with the whole world. She was still that person to a degree—working on being nicer was taking time, and to be honest, she quite liked dishing out heaps of sarcasm.

Damon now knew everything about her—she'd been good at keeping secrets throughout their relationship, guilt riddling her about it, too, until she'd confessed all her truths to him—and together they held the biggest one between them: him helping her to accept that although she'd killed a man, she wasn't evil. Acknowledging that had gone some way to her burying the past in an altogether more decent manner. That she was a murderer was something Damon was prepared to keep hidden—for her, and also because if he admitted knowing about it and hadn't reported her, he was basically an accessory, albeit a long time after the fact.

When she thought about it like that, she realised the gravity of their situation all over again. That was why he encouraged her to forget it, look to the future. No good came of picking scabs off old wounds.

"Here we are," she said, glad to be shovelling that particular pile of shite under the carpet that bore the lumps of all her other misdemeanours. "What a name, Goose Close."

Number thirty-eight stood alone at the top of an arc, forming the apex of a horseshoe of homes. It was probably a four-bed, plenty of windows going on at the front, and it had two garages, one either side. An open-plan garden consisted of grass split down the middle by a gravel path, and a gnarled tree minus its leaves stood naked to the right.

They walked to the front door. The window on left had light behind the curtains, so maybe they'd shut them before going away and had left a lamp on to deter burglars. Damon knocked, and a tabby cat appeared from somewhere, winding itself around his ankles. Stray hairs clung to the material of his trousers.

The door opened, and a man appeared, greying sideburns. Tracy held her ID up and introduced them.

"Our colleague spoke to you earlier, sir, about us visiting," she said. "We'll need to come in."

"Has something gone on while we were away?" he asked. "The lady on the phone wouldn't say."

"If we could go inside," she urged.

Benjamin Scott took them into a kitchen-diner, where a woman sat at a glass table, her brown hair in a high bun. She looked up as they entered, a tremulous smile on her red-painted lips. She'd caught the sun more than her husband.

"Take a seat, sir." Tracy gestured to the chair beside his wife.

Benjamin did that, eyeing them warily. "What's going on?"

"I'm afraid you need to prepare yourself for some bad news," she said.

"What sort of bloody bad news?" Benjamin blustered. "Get on with it, will you?"

Fair enough. "A body we believe to be your daughter's was found in her home today."

Ivory Scott stared at Tracy, while Benjamin scraped his chair across the floor and moved to the patio doors behind him. He stared out, his back to them. If they hadn't just come home from a holiday, meaning neither of them had killed her, Tracy would have thought he was deliberately hiding his face.

"A body," he said.

"Yes." Tracy opted to plough on. "She was murdered during the night."

A shriek came out of Ivory. Then she cried, wailing, her head hanging back. She clutched her neck as though the lump that was undoubtedly in her throat was strangling her. Benjamin went to her, hands on her shoulders, digging his fingers in as if his grip on her was the only thing stopping him from falling to the floor. Tears dripped for him, too, although he didn't sob, just gazed at the wall ahead, his mind maybe full of the murder and the possibilities there, perhaps memories of his daughter's life, or nothing at all.

Tracy made them tea. She placed the cups on coasters for the couple while she and Damon sipped theirs in the awkward atmosphere. Benjamin and Ivory ignored theirs. After a while, Damon popped his and Tracy's empty cups in the sink and washed them up.

"As you can appreciate," Tracy said, needing to crack on now, "I'm going to have to ask questions."

Neither of them answered or even glanced her way.

"Do you know of anyone who would have wanted to do this to your daughter?"

This set off a fresh bout of crying from Ivory, and Tracy decided to call it a day with them. It was pointless pushing for information from people who were in no fit state to provide it. Tomorrow was another day. She arranged for the Family Liaison Officer, Julie, to call round, and once she'd arrived, Tracy and Damon gave their condolences and left. Julie would deal with any questions the couple had once the first veil of grief parted to allow coherent thought in.

Tracy drove off, determined to find the little shit who'd done this to Sara and her parents. Damon remained quiet, probably processing what they'd just witnessed, and while that had been a traumatic visit, hunger didn't care about that sort of thing. Her stomach growled, so she pulled over at the retail park and eyed the array of places they could get food. The usual suspects. KFC, Burger King, McDonald's, TFI Friday, and a doughnut shop aptly named Fill That Hole.

A lemon drizzle called her name.

"We need to eat," she said. "What do you want?"

"A doughnut, seeing as that's what you'll pick."

She nudged him with her elbow. "You know it makes sense. What sort?"

"A couple of plain iced rings will do. Not in the mood for chocolate or anything."

She got out and went inside to join the short queue. Several people worked behind the counter, and someone took her order. Tracy got her debit card out as well as her ringing phone while the woman busied herself placing their doughnuts in a white cardboard box. On the side, the word HOLE had a doughnut as the O.

"Yep, Vic, what can I do for you?"

"There's another one."

She stopped herself from swearing and held her card over the contactless area of the payment device. "Two seconds, I'm in a shop." She stuffed her card in her pocket, balanced two coffees in a cup tray on the box, grabbed it all up, and rushed off to push the door. Outside, she walked towards the car. "What the fucking hell?"

"I know." Vic sighed. "A man called Frankie Bollen called it in. He's the next-door neighbour to the deceased, Olivia Zola."

"Right, give me the address then."

He supplied it, and she filed it in her mind.

"Okay, on the way."

Damon got out and took the drinks, and Tracy sat inside, doughnuts on her lap. She tucked her phone in her pocket, and while Damon settled in, she told him the news.

"This was never going to be a normal Sunday," he said, writing the address in his notebook. He handed her a coffee.

She took it and stuck it on the dash. "No, but I did think we'd get home before six. No chance of that now. Still, eat up. She's dead, no sign of the killer, so it isn't like we need to rush, is it."

They tucked in and discussed the fact that if one more body showed up, it'd be a serial, but what was new? People round here didn't seem to want to stop at one, the greedy bastards.

Food eaten, coffee gone, she messaged Nada to tell her the latest and to get on with the usual. They both used the toilet in the doughnut place, then she drove to Olivia Zola's. A SOCO van stood outside the property, as did PC Newson. She had no clue what car Paul Dunnings drove so couldn't say if he'd arrived yet.

"Which side does Frankie Bollen live?" she asked Newson from the bottom of the drive.

He jerked his thumb to her left. "He's had a bit of a shock."

"I should imagine he has."

Tracy walked up Bollen's driveway and knocked on his door. A man answered, ginger hair much the same shade as hers, curly and wiry on top, shaved at the sides and back. He was about thirty, his skinny jeans and tight-fitting T-shirt neat and tidy.

"DI Tracy Collier and DS Damon Hanks." She held up her ID. "Can we come in for a word?" She glanced about. "Saves any neighbour's listening while you're upset."

He took them into a living room, which was sparse, bachelor-like, everything he needed, nothing he appeared to want, like knickknacks, rugs, cushions, all the stuff that created a homely effect. Each to their own.

He sat, as did Tracy, but Damon remained standing by the window. He'd write things down as well as watching the street for any signs of the killer coming back to have a nose at what was going on.

"Can you tell us what happened?" she asked Bollen.

"I nipped out—sorry, do you want a drink or anything?"

"No, thank you."

"Okay, so I nipped out to get some Coke about half one. I went in the car to Morrisons. When I got back, as I pulled up the drive, I noticed Olivia's car was at an odd angle. The right-hand front was close to the wall compared to the back end, which stuck out. Then I spotted her front door ajar, so I parked and went round to her side and called her through the gap. She didn't answer, which I thought was weird, because she usually shouts for me to come in. I called a couple more times, and when she didn't respond again, I rang her." He dragged his hands down his face.

"What then?"

"Her phone rang inside, and I knew something was wrong then. She's the type to answer it after one ring, even if she's woken up by it. So I went in." He bunched his eyes shut for a moment. "She wasn't in the living room, so I checked the kitchen. She was...she was in there, sitting at her little table. I asked her if she was okay, even though I knew she wasn't. I mean, the state of her, anyone would know she was dead. I phoned the police."

"Okay. What do you mean by 'the state of her'?"

"I can't...can't talk about that. It's fucking nasty. And what was with the stuff on the table? I don't understand."

Rather than push him to describe what he'd witnessed, Tracy left it. She'd see for herself soon enough. "Did you spot anyone in the street today who isn't usually there?"

"I didn't wake up until twelve. Had a shower. Got dressed, had a bacon sarnie, then went to Morrisons."

"What about during the night? Hear or see anything then?"

"No. I slept right through."

"I don't like asking you this, but can anyone verify that?"

He shook his head. "No, I don't have a girlfriend. The sad thing is, I'd asked Olivia out, and she said no. I took it that she had a bloke—a man's been there from time to time. Small white van."

That prodded Tracy's interest button. "Do you know his name?"

"No, she denied seeing anyone when I asked."

Why would she do that? "What does he look like?"

"I didn't take that much notice."

That would do. Just the fact the fella had a van was something to go on. "Right. We're going to nip next door. If we need to pop back again, we will. Someone will take a proper statement off you shortly, or you can give it at the station."

They showed themselves out. On the pavement, Tracy waved Quinn over as he got out of his car. A female officer was with him.

To her, Tracy said, "I want a statement off the man in there." She pointed to the door. "Frankie Bollen." She waited for the officer to enter Frankie's house. "Door-to-door, Quinn, please. I specifically want to know about a man with a small white van. He visited the victim. Possible boyfriend."

Quinn nodded and got on with it.

Tracy passed that info on to the team via a message, and she'd bet a huge list of white van owners would come up, and they'd have to check every one of them for alibis.

"Did you get a vibe it was Bollen?" she asked Damon quietly.

"No," he said.

"Me neither. Come on. Let's see what's going on here then. If it's anything like the state of Sara Scott, those doughnuts might come back out to say hello."

CHAPTER SEVEN

"Put that bloody dog in the garden while we're eating," Mum said, her large earrings swaying, the weight of them pulling down her lobes.

Dad rose from the table in the dining part of the kitchen.

Mike followed him to the back door and whispered, "Dot's too small to go out there all by herself. She might go under the gate and run away."

"Is that her name?" Dad asked.

Mike nodded.

"That's lovely. And don't you worry. I bought a lead, so I'll tie her to the fence post. She won't go anywhere then." Dad opened the door and whistled.

Dot bounded in from the living room, and Dad attached the collar and lead. He took her outside, and Mike waited by the door, safe there, away from Mum.

Once they were seated again, she brought the plates over. Dad and Mike had liver, mash, and onion gravy. The cabbage was sloppy and overcooked, water swimming where she hadn't drained it enough. Her plate was bursting with pizza slices. Dad stared at it. Opened his mouth to say something but changed his mind.

Mike's liver didn't look right. It wasn't brown like Dad's but dark red. The mash was pink in places, blood seeping up from the plate into it.

The phone rang, and Dad shot up to get it.

"That'll be your mother," Mum said to him. "Calling to put the boot in again, same as she always does when she's been here."

Mike's birthday hadn't been the best. Now there might be a row to listen to once Dad had finished on the phone.

He looked at the liver.

"That's your punishment," Mum whispered while Dad spoke to whoever had rung. "Eat it, go on. If

you don't, you know what will happen. Nice name for the dog, by the way. Dot, isn't it?"

He knew exactly what she was saying, and his tummy rolled over. She'd get the compass and hurt Dot if he didn't eat all his dinner. Mike dug his fork in the top of the mash, putting off the inevitable of eating the bloodied bits.

Dad put the phone down. "I have to go. It's my gran."

"What about her?" Mum picked a piece of pepperoni off her pizza.

"In hospital. See you when I see you." He dashed out.

"But I'm meant to be going out with Gabby," she screeched.

The front door slammed.

Mike didn't feel well.

"Fucker," she mumbled. "Now, get on with eating." She stared at Mike. "I'll feed your dad's to Dot." She laughed. "The dinner's in the dog. I've always wanted to say that." She got up and put Dad's plate on the floor. "She can have it when she comes in—after you've eaten every speck."

Mike heaved throughout. He couldn't chew the liver properly, and chunks slid down his throat. The taste was worse raw, like when he hurt himself and sucked the blood off a scrape on his finger. His stomach kept cramping, squeezing, as if it wanted to push the food back out. And the cabbage...so snotty.

He hated her, and those stupid earrings of hers. Didn't she realise how daft they looked? One day, he'd show her. Put her ears so close to her eyes she wouldn't fail to see them.

Dinner eaten, his belly distended, Mike was allowed to let Dot in. The pup enjoyed Dad's dinner, and Mum laughed a bit too hard at the fact Dad would go hungry.

Gabby arrived then, entering in a cloud of Chanel No.5, her heels clacking on the kitchen tiles. "Hi, Mikey. Happy birthday!"

She'd remembered, and a glow lit him up inside.

"Where's your daddy?" Gabby asked.

"He's in the loo," Mum butted in. "Let's go then."

Gabby ruffled Mike's hair. "See you, Scamp."

They left, the door closing tight, and Mike stood there and cried. There was no one here but Dot, and it was dark outside—anyone could come in and get him, hurt him.

He scooped his doggy into his arms and ran upstairs to be sick. Then he hid under the bed, Dot beside him, and after a good old cry, he fell asleep, hoping Dad would be back by the time he woke up.

CHAPTER EIGHT

As Frankie had said, Olivia sat at the kitchen table. Her hair had been hacked off and draped over her shoulders. Thankfully, there was no excessive blood—her arm hadn't been sliced. She had a plate of food in front of her—mashed potatoes, cabbage, onion gravy, and the most disturbing thing? That raw liver again.

She was slumped, her chin to her chest, head tilted to one side, and fingermark bruising was evident on her neck. Arms dangling loosely at her sides gave the impression she'd had everything sucked out of her, nothing inside her skin to keep her rigid. Her clothes were intact apart from her T-shirt, which had been cut down the middle to reveal the dots, four drawn-on windows, and a door. No prizes for working out what that picture would be. This time, a book of dot to dot wasn't here, but the page relating to Olivia's torso was. It didn't have holes or blood on it so couldn't have been used as a template. It was a house, and it had been coloured in, rough, as though done quickly.

Had the killer created that prior to coming here, or had they brought their coloured pencils with them and done it, maybe while Olivia sat in pain, or more hideously, after she was dead?

The sky wasn't blue but black, a streak of lightning white and jagged down the middle. Far from its usual cheery yellow, the sun was red, an angry face on it. Instead of wavy sunrays, knives stuck out with blood on the blades. People had been drawn behind the windows—a boy and a man—and in the front garden, three crosses stood lurching, giving it the feel of a cemetery.

Tracy's stomach knotted at that. Had three people been killed and they'd only found two? Or were those graves from deaths in the past? She peered closer. Each cross had 'Dot' written on it.

"Look at that," she said to Damon.

He leant over. "Three people called Dot, dead? That's a bit odd."

"It is, but it's also a link to the book at Sara's, this page here, and the dot-to-dot images on the torsos. Most people will draw a house with a blue sky, maybe a few white clouds, a yellow sun, and a garden with flowers in it. Some even add curtains. The typical family household. Those who deviate too much from that usually have issues. There's a man and kid here. Father and son? Abuser and abused? Where's the mother? Has her absence played a part in how the one we're after behaves?"

"Or do we have a female killer, and the two males represent whatever to her? Husband and son, two brothers, an uncle and cousin."

Tracy studied Olivia again. "Lots of possibilities, and we *could* be looking for a woman." She nodded at Olivia. "Those earlobes have been attached to her eyelids this time."

The pressure of a staple gun had made quite a mess. She was minus her eyebrows, the same as Sara, and again, they'd been placed beneath her nose. Why were those lobes significant? Why did the victims need to have a moustache?

She thought about one of Bethany Smith's cases she'd reviewed. Some nutter had gone around Shadwell murdering, and drawing a moustache had meant something to the killer. She couldn't remember what it was so would look at that file again to check—if she remembered.

Paul Dunnings came in, standing beside Damon. "Bit messy, this one." He pointed to Olivia's eyes. "Can't find a stapler anywhere."

"Killer probably took it," Tracy said.

"Something I noticed at Sara's scene as well as here..." Paul lowered his mask with the back of his wrist. "Neither of them has a toothbrush."

"So they must have been removed," she said.

"Sara had some spare heads for an electric one, and the charging base was still in her bathroom." Paul shook his head. "To take them as trophies is a bit odd."

"To do *this* to them is a bit odd," she said, indicating Olivia. "Anything else?"

"Regarding the meal: no potato peel in the bin, no remnants of cabbage, no liver packaging. Likewise, no onion skin. I'd say the meal was prepared elsewhere and put on the plate here."

Damon cleared his throat. "Raw liver at Sara's, too, on the sofa. Any Space Raiders or rice around?"

"Not as far as I've seen," Paul said. "But you might want to come and look at something upstairs."

They followed him out of the kitchen and into the hallway. Gilbert stepped inside, minus Kathy, thank God, and he smiled.

"Interesting nugget for you, Tracy." Gilbert secured his booties. "Seems Sara's nails were cleaned with toothpaste. Kathy scraped some out from beneath them. At least we assume it's toothpaste, going by the peppermint smell."

Paul looked at Tracy.

"The toothbrushes," she said. "So we assume the nails have been cleaned with them because Sara and Olivia scratched the killer. Someone could be walking around with marks on them."

"Makes sense," Gilbert said. "Kathy will be dealing with Sara now, so we'll soon know if all the skin was removed from beneath the nails. We might get lucky and have a small amount left behind. Anyhow, where's the body?"

"The kitchen," Tracy said. "We'll be with you in a few. Just got to look at something upstairs."

Gilbert ambled off, and his, "Oh, bloody hell's bells!" followed them up the steps.

Tracy couldn't help but smile. It was better than crying.

In the main bedroom, Paul put his face mask back up and stood to the side of a white chest of drawers. "This isn't normal."

Tracy and Damon went over there. Several earrings had been placed in pairs side by side, from smallest to largest. Beneath the big garish ones, ears with elongated lobes had been drawn in black felt tip—the same one used to put the dots on the victims? The word STUPID had been written below, and it appeared that a stencil had been used to create the letters. At the other end, the smaller ones had been deemed PRETTY AND ACCEPTABLE.

"Um, no, not normal at all," Tracy said. "Whoever this is, they don't appear to like earrings bigger than a penny."

"Maybe that's why the bottoms of the ears were cut off. To make a point," Damon said.

"Who to? The victim?" She blew out a sigh. "Sort of like: Okay, I'm going to kill you, but first, you need to know I don't dig your earrings, and to show you how much, I've got a pair of scissors here..." She shuddered. "Sick fucker."

"There's more." Paul moved over to the double wardrobe and opened the doors.

"Oh." Tracy's heart skipped a beat, and her legs wobbled.

The thing had been attached to a coat hanger and hung from the rail, facing them, a mannequin of sorts, fashioned out of clothes stuffed into American tan tights. The head...well...

"Is that *skin* for the face?" She took a step closer.

Yep, a face had been crudely stitched together in patches with black thread, as though the skin had been removed from a few raw chicken thighs. Eyes were green olives secured with cocktail sticks, and the mouth was a sweetie, red lips, kept in place the same way. It didn't have a nose.

"Looks like some of Olivia's hair on that head," she murmured.

"It's sick, all of it," Damon said.

"Too bloody right."

Arms poked out of an unbuttoned, short-sleeved blouse—cream, silk. Legs dangled from the holes of denim shorts, red high-heeled shoes on the ends, held on with cable ties. A page from a dot-to-dot book covered the torso, and the puzzle had been completed. The image was of a dog, RIP x 3 scrawled beside it.

"Same as the crosses on the other picture," she said. "Three deaths."

Paul hummed. "Victims, or does this refer to the dog?"

"That's something we'll have to work out, although how, with nothing else to go on, I don't know," she said.

"See that just there?" Damon pointed to the corner of the picture. "The writing's really tiny, but it says: DON'T CALL MY DOT SKANKY, YOU BITCH.

"What the fuck?" Tracy was getting a bit arsey, to be honest. "Are you sure that says 'dot' and not 'dog'?"

"Nope, definitely a T," Damon said.

"So who is Dot?" she mused. "I'll send that info to Nada, see if she can find anything. There might be people called that who need speaking to." She took her phone out and passed the message on.

Nada: OKAY. OLIVIA'S NEXT OF KIN IS KAREN ZOLA, HER MOTHER. LIVES IN EXETER. I'LL GET ON TO THE STATION THERE, ASK THEM TO VISIT HER.

Tracy: THANKS. DO THAT, THEN GET ON WITH THIS DOT BUSINESS.

She put her mobile away again. "Is that it for this afternoon's dose of strange?" she asked Paul.

"It's all we've found so far."

"Right, we'll nip down and see Gilbert." She led the way, relieved his sidekick was busy with Sara. In the kitchen, she found him writing on his clipboard. "Same method of death, do you reckon?"

"Hello again, you two. Yes, strangulation. With Sara, though, it wouldn't have taken long—she'd suffered great blood loss prior to death. I wonder why this lady's wasn't drained and used to create alarming artwork?"

"Time? The killer could have been tired?" Damon said.

"Or worried about being spotted leaving the property? Or maybe there's some method to their madness that will become evident as the hours pass." What Tracy didn't say was: *When another body turns up.*

"No blunt force to the head, so she was strangled while conscious—unless there's a drug in her system we've yet to discover, but toxicology will let us know on that score." Gilbert sniffed. "Likewise with Sara. This earlobe business, though... What pushes people to do this sort of thing?"

"Trauma," she said, knowing from experience. "People who feel forced to kill, or compelled to...there's usually an underlying reason, and trauma is the culprit."

Damon coughed. A warning: *Don't say too much.*

She nodded at him to acknowledge it, giving him a glare that said: *I'm not fucking stupid.*

"While it isn't the right thing to do," she went on, "for the killer, it's the *only* thing. It makes them think all the issues will go away if the object of their hate is gone." *But they don't. The bastards stay with you.*

"The posing at the dinner table. Hmm." Gilbert took his temperature device out and got on with that.

"A memory, something that caused pain, either physically or emotionally," she said. "Or the event may be linked to something prior to it, or after, and this meal is important, a pivotal point. Dare I say it, but do people still eat liver and mash nowadays? The younger generations, I mean. Has it been overtaken by the more appealing dinners?"

"I take it you don't like liver," Gilbert said.

"Absolutely not. We had to make faggots at school once. I don't even want to tell you the mess the machine made of the liver, and the smell…" She held back a heave. The mushed-up liver had been a mass of pulpy red. Thinking of it gave her a newfound respect for Gilbert and what he had to deal with in his job.

"Can't beat Mr Brain's faggots," Damon said. "Always wondered as a kid whether they were made out of brains because Mr Brain made them."

"And you ate them anyway? Weirdo. Well, you'll be scoffing them on your own if you ever get any in with the weekly shop," she grumbled. "I've been put off them for life. What gets me is the liver in both cases has been raw. Look at it on that plate. The mash has soaked up the blood. And who takes the time to make this meal, package it, then bring it here to dish up? Hang on…" She moved to the kitchen area and checked the cupboards. "Okay, that's her plate. It's the same as the stack over here. I got all excited then, thinking it was the killer's."

"Sorry to break up this delightful conversation…" Gilbert put the temp device away. "She died between six and eight this morning. Given that it's a Sunday, good luck with finding any of the neighbours awake during those hours."

"I suppose we'd better go out there, see if Quinn and his partner need some help with that." Tracy sighed. "At least the next of kin visit is down to someone else this time. See you, Gilbert."

"Tarra," he said.

They left the house, taking their protectives off and popping them in a large evidence bag. PC Newson held out the log, and Tracy signed it, as did Damon. On the pavement, she looked up and down the street. Quinn stood outside a house opposite, and the officer who'd gone in to take Bollen's statement wasn't around—she was probably still in there.

Quinn walked towards them. "I've done the three neighbours on each side, bar Mr Bollen, plus five over the road—they're the most likely to have seen or heard something. No one did, so I'll get on with the others now."

"When that uniform comes out of Bollen's, get her to help you. What's her name?"

"Michelle Bradbury," Quinn said. "Started last month."

"That explains why I don't know her then. Right, we need to be getting back to the station for a catch-up with the team, so let me know if anything happens here."

She got in the car with Damon and drove away. "This has got to be the weirdest case yet."

"I don't know, we've had a fair few."

"True. You thought I was going to slip up with Gilbert, didn't you? About me killing—"

"What have I told you? Don't say the words unless we're at home and you have to get something off your chest."

"Sorry." She was. "But you did think I'd mention it, didn't you?"

"It's always there, in my head, so I have to make sure you don't blab by accident. I don't want you banged up."

"And I don't want you banged up either. This is why I *don't* say anything. It's inevitable I'm going to discuss why people kill, because that's my job, so try not to panic. And it's true, what I said. Trauma set this lot in motion. Somewhere out there is a damaged person. They could have mental issues or they could be just like me—someone who wanted justice, and a prison term for the victims isn't enough."

"But Sara and Olivia are unlikely to have done anything to warrant death instead of a sentence."

"How do we know? Just because they haven't got records, doesn't mean they weren't hideous to someone and caused them pain. Anyway, I sense this discussion will send us into argument territory, so let's just shut up about it." She slid into her space in the station car park and got out.

They walked up the stairs to the incident room in silence. She gave his hand a squeeze before going in—*sorry for being a bitch*, her usual apology—then went over to the coffee machine to pour them both a cup. The rest of the team had drinks, so she handed Damon his and stood in front of the whiteboards.

"Okay, stop what you're doing and listen up." She told them about Olivia's scene, then, "Same killer, obviously. What did you lot find out regarding Sara's friends?"

Tim pulled his notebook across his desk towards him. "That's easy. We split up and took a few each. None of them have any grudges against her. All said she was lovely. As far as they know, there's no reason for anyone to kill her."

Lara drank some coffee then put the cup beside her keyboard. "One of them mentioned a third man she was seeing."

"Ooh, that's interesting," Tracy said. "Did you get a name?"

"No. The woman said Sara never told her who he was, just that he came by in the middle of the night, used the key. What she did say was he kept asking Sara to hug him like a child—you know, on her lap. He wanted his head stroked and for her to say: You're a good boy. I love you and I'm proud of you."

Tracy frowned. "So either someone with a harmless fetish or he needs the love of a mother." She thought about the picture of the house. "Like I said, a man and boy had been drawn in the windows—no mum. Are we searching for someone who's mum died and they're missing her?"

"*Missing* her?" Alastair said. "More like harbouring immense rage regarding her. Got to be, to kill like that and do all that weird stuff to them."

Erica nodded. "I agree. The mother is possibly absent for a reason, and the son—if it is a male doing this—has issues about it."

"Okay," Tracy said. "I want two of you in Sara's street, asking the neighbours if they've ever been awake during the night and spotted a third man going into the house. Did Sara give her friend a description of him?"

Lara nodded. "Said he wasn't her usual type. Slim, tall, whereas she usually goes for stocky."

"That's true with Ted Underby. Did anyone get anywhere with Jacob Mannings?"

Tim tapped his pen on his head. "Yep. He hasn't been to Sara's for a while—he's got what he terms a 'proper girlfriend' now."

"As opposed to someone he just visits for sex?" Tracy asked.

"Yes. He reckons the last time he used the key at Sara's was a couple of months ago. He didn't have a specific date but said he could possibly narrow it down when he's had time to think about it."

"Where was he last night?"

"At a family do. Hired hall. About seventy witnesses," Tim said. "His brother was there when I called round. He confirmed the party."

"Fair enough. We'll leave him alone for now then." She turned to the whiteboards. "I see you've all added your info, so that just leaves me to add mine. Oh, Nada, did you get anything on 'Dot'?"

"Several Dorothys around, all old. Erica's been ringing them for a chat."

Tracy looked at her. "Anything?"

Erica shook her head and sighed. "Sadly not. None of them have heard of Sara or Olivia."

"Rightio." Tracy picked up the pen to add her information. "Everyone get on with the usual. If we've found nothing by four, we'll call it a day. We might all get a roast dinner in yet."

CHAPTER NINE

Val wasn't in the best of moods. She'd been asked to work later than her usual stopping time of two. Percy, the old boy who'd started last month, had called in sick for his afternoon shift. More than likely he was in Sunday mode and couldn't be arsed to come in. As usual, Val was the first to be pressured into staying on.

Her boss, Mr Lays, always had her feeling like she couldn't say no. It was his manner, she reckoned, all puffed out chest and stern stares. Of course, Val had taken over one of Percy's hours, and now it was three o'clock, she scooted into the staffroom to get the hell out so Mr Lays didn't ask her to remain at the till until four. Mind you, the shop wasn't even that busy, so the other staff could deal with the customers.

Coat on, her bag hanging on her shoulder, she left Sainsbury's via the front entrance, walking round to the rear staff car park. She could have gone through the back way, but Sevah, the bloke who stacked the pallets in the delivery bay, gave her the sodding creeps. Always looking at her funny, especially at her boobs.

Bloody pervert.

She drove away, so glad to be going home. Tomorrow was her day off, and she usually spent it with her sister. They got their nails painted, had a mooch around town, then ate lunch somewhere, which extended well into the afternoon if they sank a few glasses of wine. Val needed tomorrow badly. She'd worked double shifts most of the week so was tired.

In front of her house, she left the car and glanced down at the road outside Anne's. That was weird. It had rained earlier, coming down in a massive whoosh, sudden and without warning, the customer she'd been serving commenting on it while watching it lash onto the store's floor-to-ceiling windows. Then the sun had emerged as if the rain hadn't just overtaken its job of lighting the world.

A dry rectangle where a vehicle had been parked in front of Anne's meant someone had left their car there while it had rained, then left afterwards. The shower had lasted about five minutes, so maybe it was one of those delivery drivers and they'd decided to sit until it had passed. It had to be that, because no one ever parked in front of Anne's otherwise.

Val shrugged, too weary to give it any more thought. Up her path she went, sliding her key in the lock, taking her time about it in case Anne nipped out for a chat. Val liked her and hoped she'd be able to help her with the PTSD in future. She thought their chats helped. After all, it was always in their gardens, and that got Anne out of the house, even if only for ten or fifteen minutes.

Anne's door was ajar, so Val opened her own and dumped her bag in the hallway. Then she turned to the dividing fence and leant over. "Anne? Are you coming out for a natter? If you are, shall I make us a drink?"

Anne didn't like having anyone in her house, nor did she enjoy visiting other people. Something about needing to be home, alone, so she could be safe and not feel cornered. Val or Anne made cuppas for when they chatted, and it was Val's turn. She had some nice coffee sachets in her bag she'd picked up cheap from work—the box had been squashed so wasn't out on the shelf for sale—and she'd only need to add boiled water.

"Anne, love, are you there?"

With no response, Val grew jittery. Her stomach dropped. What if that fella had got out of prison early and had come for her? Joseph Ward or something. Definitely Joseph anyway. Or what if Anne had one of her episodes and blacked out, banging her head?

"Bloody hell…" Val wasn't sure what to do. If she went into Anne's, it might set her neighbour off on one, and the last thing Val wanted was to put Anne two steps backwards in her recovery. Still, her not answering was a worry.

Val went inside her own house first to stick the kettle on. Anne could be in the toilet next to the front door, for God's sake, and had left it ajar to let Val know she needed to talk. That didn't mesh with Anne's usual behaviour, though, so Val rushed outside, down her path and up Anne's. On her step, she said, "Anne? Are you all right?"

No answer.

Sod it, I'm going to have to go in whether she likes it or not.

Val nudged the door with her elbow and walked into the hallway. Everything appeared fine, so she checked the kitchen. Anne wasn't there, but a cup of tea sat on the table. She went over and touched the side of it—cold, just like Val's skin had gone.

Something was wrong for Anne to have left her drink.

Shaking and calling out to her friend, she returned to the hallway. The living room door was shut, so she turned the knob and went inside.

"Oh. Oh my fucking *God!*"

Anne was on the floor, her legs wide, her top open, showing her chest and belly. She had spots all over it. Was that a side-effect of anxiety? Hives, wasn't it? No, that couldn't be right. Something had been drawn on her, but Val couldn't make out what it was from this distance.

"Anne?" she said, hoping she'd get some kind of response, at the same time knowing she'd hear nothing but her own breathing, laboured from panic. "*Anne!*"

Oh, what the hell was that on her eyes?

Val backed away, ferreting in her pocket for her phone. She went outside, unable to stand being in the house anymore, and jabbed at her screen, ringing the police. Once she'd said what she thought had happened, she cut the call. She couldn't bear to stay on the line like she'd been asked. Her head was too full of gross images for her to take in whatever the person on the other end of the connection had wanted to say.

Leaning against the fence, she took a moment to catch her breath, then had the awful thought that whoever had done that to Anne might still be in her bloody house. Val legged it down the path and along hers, going inside and locking herself in. She felt awful for leaving Anne like that, with the door wide open because she hadn't thought at the time to pull it to, but distancing herself from the horrors was all she could think about.

"Coffee," she said, as if that would make everything okay again. It wouldn't, but the act of making it would take her mind off...off *that*.

She tipped the sachet contents into a cup and added the now boiled water. Tears stung at the fact the coffee was supposed to be for both of them to sip on while they tried to put Anne's world to rights. Now what? Anne was dead—Val didn't want to admit that, but she had to—and it was all that Joseph man's fault. If he was still in prison, Val would bet he'd sent someone else to do the dirty work. She'd be telling the police that an' all.

A set of knocks had her almost dropping her cup in fright. She placed it on the worktop and went to answer, checking though the peephole first. A police officer stood there, another in Anne's garden approaching the house.

Val opened the door.

"Hello. I'm Simone York. You rang about your friend being hurt?"

Was that what Val had said? That Anne was hurt? She couldn't remember. "I don't think she's hurt. I think she's *dead*." She shivered at saying it out loud.

"Can I just come in and talk about it?" York asked.

Val stepped back, so glad to have someone else there to take responsibility for everything but at the same time wishing this wasn't happening. She led the woman to the kitchen and picked up her cup to give her something to do. York stared at it.

"Oh, would you like one?" Val asked. "It's only that instant stuff. Cappuccino."

"That would be lovely, thanks."

Val got on with making it.

"Can you tell me how you came to find your neighbour?"

Val stirred the coffee then handed it over. She explained Anne's anxiety issues and how they chatted over the fence. "So I thought her leaving the door open was for that, although it was highly odd for her to do it. Leave it open, I mean."

"Why's that?"

Val lifted her coffee and sipped. "Because there's an ex in the picture. Well, not in the picture as such—he's in prison. He used to beat her up, and that's why he's in there."

"I see. Did Anne feel he would come and get her then?"

"Wouldn't you? Some nutter gives you a wallop, gets put inside, and you think it'll be okay now? Anne has PTSD from his abuse. She has trouble leaving the house. She can't work and has everything delivered."

"She was forced into being a recluse?" York asked.

"Yes."

"So what happened when you went inside?"

Val told her, shuddering at having to explain what she'd seen.

"Did you touch anything?"

"Yes, the front door, the cup in the kitchen, and the handle on the living room door." That was wrong, wasn't it? She shouldn't have done that, but how was she to know what she'd stumble into?

"Oh..." York put her cup on the table. "I just need to contact the front desk about what you saw."

Val sipped while York left the kitchen and did that, the drink heating her tummy, bringing warmth back to her skin. York returned, and Val finished her story.

"Do you have anyone who can sit with you for a while?" York asked. "You've had a bit of a shock."

"A bit is an understatement. There was something else. A car had been parked outside Anne's—and that's unheard of. Everyone respects her need to be able to see clearly if anyone's coming, so whoever was there isn't from this street."

"Did you see the vehicle?"

"No, but it had rained, and there was a dry patch on the road."

After a few more questions, York finished her coffee then left the house, asking Val to stay indoors until a detective called Tracy came round. Val wasn't going anywhere. She threw the bolts across the front door then rang her sister, crying. That always happened, didn't it? You were fine until you phoned a loved one and heard their voice.

Val choked back a sob, upset she'd never hear Anne's again.

Simone York stared at the dry patch on the road, which had probably got bigger now the rain was drying up. She glanced around to see which people were most likely to have seen something if they'd looked out of their windows. She nipped up Anne's path and called out to Robbie Upworth, the lad she was on shift with today.

"You okay in there?"

"Yeah. Deceased. The rest of the house is clear," he said.

"Did you put booties on?" The last thing Simone wanted was Tracy Collier in her face for that mistake.

"Yes, once I established we had a body, not an injury."

Okay, Robbie should get away with that, especially as the call had come in that someone was hurt, not dead.

"All right. I'm going to start house-to-house. According to the woman who found her, someone was parked outside earlier. We need to find out who that is."

"Obviously..."

He sounded naffed off with her and, as usual, that niggle of doubt burrowed into her tummy. Simone wasn't cut out for this job, and whether it was her nerves around Collier or the prospect of always getting a bollocking off her no matter what she did, she couldn't settle into her role. Well, this time, she'd show Collier she could take the initiative, get the ball rolling before time pressed on. It'd show Robbie, too, who was a bit of a know-it-all and someone she didn't like working with. Newson was her favourite beat partner.

She tried the house to the right of Anne Walton's. A middle-aged man answered, peering over at the police car then back to her. It appeared he'd been asleep.

"Hello, sir. I'm enquiring as to whether you heard or saw anything today that might be considered strange." That hadn't sounded right. Why couldn't she ask questions properly? 'Strange' could mean anything. "What I mean is, did you hear anything coming from next door?" She thumbed towards Anne's. "An argument perhaps?"

"I never hear anything from Anne. She's lovely and quiet. Besides, I was asleep, and once my head hits the pillow, I'm out of it. Nothing will wake me up bar my alarm. I've been at work. Night shift." He went on to explain his profession.

She wrote down where he was employed. "So when did you wake up?"

"Five minutes ago. Haven't even had a chance to drink me tea or have me shower. Why? Something happened, has it?"

"Did you see a car parked outside Anne's?"

"What, in me dreams?" He snorted. "No."

"What time did you go to work?"

"I left here about eight last night to start for half past."

"Did you see anyone then?"

"Only Anne. She was at her window, looking out. Not unusual for her. She sits there nearly all the time."

"Okay, thank you."

Simone left him to wake up properly and opted for the house directly opposite Anne's. No sooner had she raised her hand to knock than the door flew open.

"Woss going on?" a burly woman asked, her grey hair in rollers beneath a stretchy brown net. She was about seventy and almost filled the frame. "Is it that fella come back to get her?"

She must be referring to the one Val mentioned. Shit. I didn't ask Val what he was called.

"Which man is that?" Simone asked.

"That bloody Joseph Vord. Always was a little git, even as a kid. I said to my Stan that he'd end up in the nick, and I was right."

"How do you know Mr Vord?"

"We lived near him when he was a nipper. The shitbag used to throw stones at my Dave, which isn't in the slightest bit normal."

"Dave?"

"My old cat."

"Right. What's your name, please?"

"Elsie Fordenham."

Simone jotted that on her pad. "Did you see anyone parked outside Anne's earlier?"

"Matter of fact I did." Elsie folded her arms. "I told Stan it couldn't be a neighbour. We all know not to do that to Anne. It'd set her off."

"Did Stan see it, too?"

The woman laughed. "Stan's dead, love. I just talk to him. Saves me feeling alone."

Simone swallowed the sudden lump in her throat. "I'm so sorry. The car then. Did you—?"

"It weren't no car. It was a van. White. One of them small kinds. A bloke got out of it, all dressed up in a uniform, he was. A bit like yours, except he didn't have a police hat, which I thought was odd. He had a cap on. Long, straggly hair, brown, and a bugger of a moustache. Big thing. I'd say he was in his thirties."

"Okay, that's been very helpful. Did you notice what time he arrived?"

"No, but it was after lunch. I'd just finished me sausage and brown sauce sarnie. The van was there for a good while. Weird thing was, he was talking to her at the door—she had the chain on, nothing unusual there—but what *was* unusual was she let him in."

Simone thought back to Val saying about Anne never letting anyone inside. "Did he force himself in?"

"No. He had some papers and showed them to her, and a short while after that, she opened up, although she did look worried. I had it in mind to go over there, see if she was okay, but my son phoned, so I got caught up in that instead."

Shit. "Okay, is there anything else you'd like to add?"

"Only that for you lot to be here, something's got to have happened."

To stop herself divulging information, Simone said goodbye and tried the neighbours either side of Elsie's. Neither had seen anything. She was just about to go to another house when a SOCO van trundled down the street, closely followed by Collier and Hanks. Simone realised too late that she'd fucked up. She should have cordoned off the area where the van had parked, plus Anne's garden.

Her heart sank.
Best prepare myself to get barked at then.

CHAPTER TEN

Mike's nap had revived him, and, in a bold move, he reckoned he'd take Dot out for a spin. She jumped around him once she spied her lead, and he clipped it to her light-pink collar, laughing.

"You're a daft girl," he said, ruffling the top of her head. "Let's go to all the places, shall we?"

He took her down the alley to the garage. She leapt in the back seat of his car, panting and whining, silly and excited, the soppy thing. Mike smiled at her and got in. He drove through the estate then on to the main road opposite Sara's, not intending to stop; it would just be nice to see what was going on. A large van was in her street, and a tent had been placed in front of the door. A copper stood there, talking to someone in a white outfit, nodding and gesturing.

So they'd found her then.

Mike moved on, thinking about whether one of her other fellas had visited after he'd left. God, he'd have loved to have seen that. The shock, the horror that Peggy was dead and she'd never open her legs to them again. The uncomfortable thought of Mike himself being like them, doing rude things with Peggy when she'd been Sara, left him unsettled.

He didn't want to think about the connotations of that.

On he went, towards Olivia's, but he couldn't get down her road. For some reason, the whole street had been cordoned off, not just outside her house, which he'd see if he craned his neck, which he didn't. He wasn't fond of jarring it. She'd been discovered, too. Who by? It bugged him that he didn't know. There was a van there, too; must be something to do with the police.

So he didn't raise anyone's suspicions, he continued to Anne's, then stopped at the T-junction, just before he'd normally turn into her street. Lots of activity there as well—two coppers in uniforms at doors, a van again, and a red-haired woman talking to a man on the pavement.

Mike shot off, glad he'd used his car and not the work van, and he let his mind wander. Val would have been the one to stumble upon Anne, and he'd intended for that to happen. The more people who knew how bad Peggy was, the better, and it seemed Val liked to talk, so she'd be spreading it around that Peggy being killed served her right, and that would be the truth, the fucking dirty leg-spreader. If this made the news, then everyone in town would know she was a slag. Maybe he'd get lucky and the nationals would get in on it, then the whole country and other parts of the world would be told about Peggy and how she'd forced him to eat that liver. The police would understand, wouldn't they, why he'd left those things at the houses? Why he'd splashed Sara's blood everywhere?

With Dot whimpering for a wee, he took her to the small forest and let her out. Not the forest he'd avoided for years—well, that was the woods really, but he hadn't been there since a few weeks after…after he'd done something there.

Dot ran ahead while he ambled, in no rush, and thought about who'd be next. He reckoned he'd pick Dierdre Kaggle, a woman who resembled what Peggy would have looked like had she lived to that age. Using the High Court enforcement agent angle again would be good. He'd do it tomorrow, once she was back from taking her boxer for its morning trot. Her neighbours all worked, she didn't, and as there were only five houses in the little close, there'd be nothing to worry about.

Happy he'd made a firm decision, he sat on a tree stump while Dot sniffed the bases of trunks and darted around. She was his world, and he loved her so much his chest grew tight if he thought about it too much.

Nothing beat a dog as your best friend.

Mike woke, forgetting for a moment he was under the bed. Dot snuffled his ear, her nose wet and cold, and he remembered then, why he was there. Mum had gone out with Gabby, leaving him and Dot alone, and Dad was at the hospital because his gran was poorly.

Mike's stomach grumbled, and that wasn't surprising. He'd been sick after that liver, hadn't he, so his belly was empty. If he could just get down to the kitchen without being too scared, he could make a jam sandwich. He crawled out, the carpet wiry on his palms, the hard fibres digging into his fingertips.

Dot waddled along behind him to the landing, her body all chubby and puppyish, and they descended the stairs, Mike's heart hurting from it beating so hard. At the bottom, he paused, listening in case Mum and Dad were back and he just didn't know it. But no, the hallway was dark, so he continued to the kitchen. The light beneath one of the wall cupboards gave off just enough glow for him to see what he was doing, and he set about spreading margarine and jam on his bread, then squashing the slices together. He was naughty and took out a packet of pickled onion Space Raiders, pouring them into a small plastic bowl.

He thought about when Mum and Gabby had left. The main light had been on in the kitchen, plus the one in the hall. Why were they now off? Who had put the cupboard one on? Scaring himself at the idea of someone getting inside and messing around with the lights, he quickly cleaned the crumbs off the worktop and washed the knife, putting it away. He'd go upstairs and hide under the bed again, eat his food, then maybe get back to sleep. He held his plate and stacked the bowl on top of the sandwich.

"What are you doing, you little thief?"

Mike spun to the dining area. Shadows swarmed there, so he couldn't see too far, but he'd know that spiteful voice anywhere. "I'm sorry."

"Why have you got that food?"

"I'm hungry."

"What, after that big dinner?"

He nodded.

"You're greedy, that's what you are," she said.

It was scary, hearing her but not seeing her.

"Do you know," she said, "I had a lovely time tonight, met up with my new fella, and he told me I'm wasted by being a mother and I should go and live with him. I think he's right. I mean, who'd want to be your *mother?"*

"I don't know."

"Well, it's not me, that's for certain. And he loves my hair. Says I should never cut it off."

She didn't sound right, her words all slurry. Mike stood there shaking, the Space Raiders shushing in the bowl, and he didn't know what to say. When she was like this, after the wine, she could be meaner than usual. She might hurt Dot if he said the wrong thing, so he had to be really, really careful and think before he spoke.

"Aren't you going to eat that sandwich and those crisps then, seeing as you got up in the middle of the night to steal them?" she asked.

"If I'm allowed."

"Well, you were clearly going to eat them anyway, whether you had permission or not. Years ago, and in some countries even now, you get your hand chopped off if you nick something and get caught. I should cut your hands off. With scissors. Go and get them out of the drawer."

Mike put the bowl and plate in the side and did as she'd asked, hoping and praying she didn't cut his hands off. He took the scissors to her, imagining the pain, and tears stung his eyes.

The scrape of a key going in the lock had Mike sagging with relief and Mum gasping.

"Quickly, put those scissors down," she said.

He ran over and threw them on the draining board, and the sight of them would stay in his head forever, he reckoned. They'd been so close to cutting him.

"Not fucking ready for this at all," Mum mumbled, "but it has to be done. Come and sit over here in the dark. There's something you need to see and hear."

Mike picked up his plate and bowl and walked into the dining room, squinting in an attempt to see where she was. There, on the floor in the corner, but she was getting up now and teetered.

"Watch and learn," she whispered, her wine breath vile and hot. "And not a word that you're here. You know what I'll do if you let your dad know you're watching and listening, don't you?"

Mike nodded, but she might not be able to see that, so he said quietly, "Yes."

She didn't say "Good boy" as he prayed she would, and he supposed he ought to stop hoping for that really. Instead, she staggered into the kitchen and leant against the sink unit, arms across her tummy. Dot scampered over from the kitchen area and pressed herself to Mike's leg. She didn't like being near Mum—she was learning fast. The front door closed, and Mike imagined Dad resting back on it, staring at Mum opposite.

"I don't bloody believe this. Did you go out?" Dad sounded well angry.

"Of course I bloody did. What, did you think I'd spend all that time getting ready and not bother? You're off your trolley if you think that."

"No, not off my trolley, just thinking that as I was at the hospital, our son would need looking after. Please tell me you got a babysitter." Dad came in and gave her the once-over. He didn't seem pleased at all with his face scrunched up like that.

She waved his words away. "He was fine by himself. The dog can protect him."

"It's a puppy, not some big guard dog, not yet. Peggy, are you mental or something? You don't

leave a little kid by himself so you can go out and get pissed."

"Got more than pissed," she muttered.

"What was that?" Dad cocked his head, eyebrows going up.

Mike didn't like this. His belly hurt. To stop himself from making a noise by crying, he bit into one half of his sandwich. The jam and butter didn't taste sweet like they usually did, but bitter. Food always was when those two had an argument. Everything went rotten then.

"You heard." Mum lurched towards a wall cupboard and swung it wide. An open bag of rice fell out, landing on the worktop and spilling there and on the floor. "Now look what you've made me do."

"I think you'll find you did that by yourself."

She gave Dad the evils. "I wanted a fucking glass anyway, not food." She ferreted in the next one and took out a champagne flute, one of two they'd had as a wedding present.

"I think you've had enough, don't you?" Dad asked.

"Oh, you have no idea how true that is. Yes, I've had enough, but not wine, never that. Wine keeps me sane in this hellhole. I've had enough of you and that kid. Balls and chains, that's what you both are. I should never have agreed to marry you. Should have played the field a bit, had other men, like I've been doing for months and tonight." She breathed heavily. "And that's too late—years too late, going with men—because I've finally realised you're shit in bed as well as at everything else. All those years wasted with crappy fucks."

Mike didn't understand what fucks had to do with beds, or even what fucks were.

Dad gripped her wrist with one hand and slapped her cheek with the other. The noise it created was so loud in the middle of the night, and Mike stuffed a load of bread in his mouth to plug it up. He chewed slowly.

"You're a fucking bitch, Peggy, do you know that? A bitch. You've never cared about Mike—or me after he was born. You're just interested in acting single, going out to get drunk, and now, by your own admission, to fuck other men. You said months, but when did it start? Exactly how long has this been going on?"

"Long enough to know I want him and not you. And he's not one for kids, so thank God I won't have to pop another brat out. As he's not fond and doesn't want the hassle of a child, I won't be seeing Mike once I've left."

Mike stopped chewing. She was leaving? And he wouldn't have to see her again? His smile stretched his cheeks, but then it faded. He shouldn't be happy when Dad was so upset. And even though she was awful, she was his mum, and he shouldn't want her to go.

Dad hit her again, harder, so her head snapped to one side, and the glass went flying, crashing to the floor. Dot whined, giving their position away, and Dad stared over.

"That you, son?"

Mike filled his mouth with more bread. Dot went over to Dad then yelped.

"Shit, she's got glass in her paw." Dad scooped the puppy up and removed the slither, then put her in the hallway and shut the door. *"Where's Mike?"*

"In bed, where d'you think? It's three in the fucking morning, you thick bastard. Kids his age aren't up and about, are they, unless they've crawled down for a sandwich and some crisps."

No. She mustn't tell Dad he was here. That he was a thief.

Dad gripped her wrist once more and shoved her against the sink. She let out an oof noise, so the edge of the unit must have hurt her back. Good.

"You're a nasty piece of work, Peggy. My mum told me that, but I wouldn't listen. She said you'd ruin me, and she was right all along."

Mum laughed. *"Yeah, she's going to be pleased about this, and you know what? I don't care. I'm leaving now, so get your damn hand off me."*

Instead of doing that, Dad wrapped both around her neck. *"You fucking whore."* Squeeze. *"Slapper."* A press of his thumbs. *"Bitch."*

Mum scrabbled at his arms to try to pull him off, but Dad was strong and wouldn't let go. She scratched his skin with her long nails, and blood welled in the scrapes she'd made. That must be sore. Mike rammed two Space Raiders in his mouth, and the sound of him crunching them drowned out Mum's garbled words and Dad calling her all the names under the sun, names Mike had never heard before, especially the one beginning with C. The taste of the crisps, so sour, gave him something else to focus on. Then Dad released her, and Mum's neck was red, her face tear-streaked, that black stuff she *put on her eyelashes dribbling down her cheeks and those stupid big earrings shivering.*

Mike gritted his teeth.

"That's the one and only time you'll ever do that to me," she said, voice croaky. "I'm going, right now, and you can't stop me."

"I don't want to stop you," Dad said. "You're filthy. Disgusting. How can you behave like that when you're married and have a little boy? Don't we matter?"

"No." She pushed off the unit. "I don't think either of you ever did."

She walked over the glass, the pieces crackling beneath her shoes. In the corner where Mike was, she grabbed a suitcase he hadn't even noticed, then carried it out of the kitchen. Dot yelped again, followed by a yowl.

"Don't you fucking take this out on a defenceless animal," Dad shouted. "Who kicks a dog? Get out. Go on, fuck off. I never want to see you again."

The front door slammed.

Mike popped another Space Raider in and sucked it so he didn't make a noise.

Dad slumped over the worktop, head bent, and cried for a long time, the under-cupboard lamp sending his hair a lighter shade. Mike finished his sandwich and crisps. Then Dad cleared up the rice and glass with the dustpan and brush, tipping it into the bin. Dot came back in, leaving streaks of blood on the floor, and Dad sat her on the worktop. He checked her body, probably in case Mum had hurt her badly with that kick, and bandaged her front paw, telling her she was a beautiful doggy and the nasty lady was gone now.

Mike wished she'd 'gone' instead. He imagined that big black car he'd seen on telly once, that held coffins, and inside them were dead people. Mum should be in one of those, or better still, left in the woods without one. The bugs could scoff their heads off on her then, fill their tiny tummies with her skin and meat.

He remained in the darkness, taking it in turns to suck a crisp then run his tongue over his teeth while entertaining the creatures eating so much of her that they exploded.

He waited for ages after Dad had gone upstairs, thinking of ways to make Mum gone. He could go to her work after school and stab her. Or maybe ask her to take him for a walk down by the canal and push her in. Dad couldn't have checked to see if Mike was tucked up in bed, otherwise, he'd have come back down looking for him by now.

That hurt.

As did finding Dot dead in the garden the next day, her skin punctured with wounds from a compass. Had Mum taken Mike's one with her? He couldn't imagine her new man would have one if he didn't have any kids.

Dad buried the puppy in her favourite spot and promised to get a new Dot, murmuring about the puppy getting prodded by thorns from the bushes, so he'd have to cut them down to save the next dog being hurt.

But that wasn't how Dot had died. Mum had done it. She must have used her key to get in and let Dot out. The trouble was, Mike couldn't say that. If he did, Mum would come back and do the same to him.

He'd have to ask for a new compass, pretending he'd lost his.

Mike hated lying to Dad.

CHAPTER ELEVEN

Tracy had spoken to Anne's neighbour, Val Edmunton, who'd told her what had happened. Now she was having a chat with York, telling herself to be kind to her. York prattled on, her words tripping over themselves, Tracy's presence having an effect on her, but there were worse people York could deal with in this job, so this was good practice for her.

That was what Tracy told herself anyway, to justify how she behaved with the woman. She recalled a conversation they'd had once, when York had confessed to not being the best copper. Tracy had suggested she go for a civilian admin job within the force. York had agreed that was a good idea.

So why is she still here, in a uniform she isn't fit to wear?

"Wait." Tracy held her hand up. "*What* did you just say? Actually, no, let me repeat it: A van was outside Anne Walton's, and Val knows this because it rained and left a dry patch. Val said no such thing to me." Tracy glared at York. "So where's the fucking crime scene tape? You had plenty of time to put it up quickly when I was in there talking to Val. I might not have twigged you'd fucked up then, but now? Jesus Christ. Why didn't you put in for admin? This is exactly the reason why you shouldn't be a copper. You don't think things through. You're two steps behind when you should always, *always* be two or more ahead." Tracy ignored the fact that she fucked up a lot, but this wasn't about her. *For once.*

"I'm sorry," York said. "And I did put in for admin, but there are no vacancies."

"You can bet your last bloody quid there'll be a vacancy once I've had a word."

"I knew I'd messed up, but when you arrived, everything was going on fast with SOCO and whatever, and it went out of my head."

Tracy knew how that worked; it had happened to her quite a few times and would no doubt occur again in the future. "Do it now. If I come back out and see no tape, I'm going to have a mare, got it?"

York's expression said: *So what you just had wasn't a mare?*

Before Tracy gave in to the urge to shove York in the chest so she tumbled backwards into the road—*shit, these sorts of thoughts have got to stop*—she strutted off to the SOCO van and put on a protective suit. Damon had been yakking to a woman called Elsie Fordenham across the road, and he joined Tracy, getting a suit out of a box for himself.

"What was all that about?" he asked quietly. "I didn't hear what you said, which means no one else would have, thank God, but by your tone, I'd say you tore a strip off her. *Again.*"

Tracy nodded, drawing up the zip. "Get this. A bloody van had parked outside Anne's, and she didn't cordon it off. Not only that, and I didn't bollock her for it, but she didn't put tape across Anne's gateway. I'm telling you, one day, she's going to make a massive error, and I won't be there to put her straight."

"It's not your responsibility on cases that aren't yours. If she fluffs up on the beat, she can deal with the fallout." He reached for some gloves.

"I know that, but if she'd just apply her brain a bit more..." She snapped gloves on then picked up some booties. "Anyway, hopefully the area hasn't been compromised, although I wouldn't put it past the daft bint to have walked across that dry patch when she went to see Elsie Fordenham—and I don't want to know if she did. I'll lose my shit in a way no one has seen before."

"Bloody hell. If I haven't seen your worst yet, I dread to think what it's like. The last row with Kathy was bad enough."

Tracy recalled it well. She'd told Kathy she was a ticking bomb, and although on the outside she appeared calmer and more in control these days, there were moments, like just now, where she was ready to blow to such a degree she'd probably lose her job. Someone, one day, would report her for the way she acted. It was only a matter of time.

"Let's get on and do some work," she said. "It's closing in on dinnertime, and I'm hungry again, which doesn't bode well for my future mood. We'll have a look at the body then scoot as quickly as possible."

She stomped along the pavement to Anne's, still narked there had been another murder, officially into serial territory now. She'd been on the verge of telling the team to go home when the call had come in, but now they were back at the station, doing their usual thing, except it was a new victim.

"Get a cordon here on this bloody gate," she called to Robbie Upworth, who stood at Anne's front door. "We'll sign in first, though." She scribbled her siggy then lifted one foot to put on a bootie, placing it down inside the house. She repeated it with the second and asked a SOCO, "Where's the body?" *Christ, that was abrupt.* "Please."

"In the living room," Paul butted in, coming out of the kitchen ahead.

I wasn't fucking asking you. "Thanks."

She smiled tightly, resisting turning to see if Damon, her safety net, was behind her. Showing weakness wasn't her thing. She acted as though she was fine by herself, thank you very much, and looked to a room on her right. A few SOCOs worked inside. She entered and peered around the door.

The body was on the floor in the corner, her legs splayed, her torso on show. Yet another dot formation and numbers marked her skin, and the earlobes and eyebrows being lopped off and placed were the same as Sara and Olivia. Her hair had been cut off and rested on the floor either side of her head. Tracy took a picture of Anne's belly and sent it to Nada for her to join the dots. Then she glanced around for something different to the other scenes. At Sara's there had been excessive blood, and Olivia's was the weirdo mannequin and the earrings.

And there it was, above the fireplace, a massive drawn ear with a long lobe and the words: STOP IT, YOU WHORE-SLAPPER-BITCH.

Fuck me, someone's arsey.

She stepped towards it. "Damon, come and look at this. There's smaller writing again."

He joined her and peered to the bottom right. "*You're filthy. Disgusting. How can you behave like that when you're married and have a little boy? Don't we matter?* Blimey…"

"Anne isn't married," Tracy said. "So what the hell that means, I don't know. She hasn't got a child either. Her ex made sure that didn't happen by shoving a—"

"Nope, I don't need to know." Damon winced. "That poor woman. Not only did she go through terrible abuse, and torture by the sounds of it, but she's now been killed. The info came back from Nada on Joseph Vord, by the way. He's still inside, in solitary at the moment for using the sharpened end of a pencil to stab someone's eye out."

"He sounds like a delight."

"More like a menace to society." He pointed at the drawing. "This ear infatuation. Notice how the lobes are elongated? Think about the message left at Olivia's. Small earrings are acceptable, big ones aren't. Big ones tend to be heavy, yes? Only asking, as I haven't ever worn any myself." He grinned. "So big ones could pull down an earlobe into this shape?"

Tracy shrugged. "The killer doesn't like stretched ears. Brilliant. That tells us absolutely nothing except they're weird."

"Best to theorise."

"But when it's to do with lugholes...really? Are we honestly searching for someone who's unhappy about the way *ears* look? They've got major issues and need help, not putting in prison."

"I have to agree with you there. Prison won't do this person any good."

"Did I just hear you right?" Paul said from behind them.

Tracy and Damon turned.

"You believe people need help, not punishment?" Paul stared at Tracy over his face mask, his eyes wide.

"Don't you in certain instances?" Tracy asked.

"Um, no, I don't. When you see this sort of thing far too often"—he indicated the body—"then I'm afraid they should be locked away in a prison for hardcore criminals."

"But they're still locked away in a psychiatric hospital," Tracy said, thinking about herself and how she wasn't an evil person, she'd just so happened to have snapped one day and killed a man who had helped steal her childhood. She hoped she'd be put into a hospital if what she'd done ever came to light.

"Not good enough," Paul said. "Half of them only act mental anyway."

Oh. They were going to fall out if he kept on. He'd hit a massive nerve.

"I think you should keep your archaic, not to mention barbaric opinions to your bloody self," she snapped. "You can't look at this as black and white—no crime is black and white. Yes, three women have lost their lives, and I'm sickened by that, believe me, but..." She stopped because of his eyes. They'd gone blank; he wasn't listening. "Fuck this."

She walked out into the front garden for a bit of space. It was a contentious subject, she knew that, and to get into a heated debate about it with the new lead SOCO wasn't going to get them off to a good start. See? She was learning. Stepping away before she blew her top.

I actually want to go in there and punch his lights out.

Was this a touchy area for her because of what she'd done herself? Did she only have sympathy because she understood a troubled mind and what pushed someone to act this way?

Probably.

She couldn't recall whether she'd felt like this before she'd killed John.

Convenient, that is.

She returned inside, if only to get away from that nagging voice in her head.

Damon stood by the living room door. "Paul's just mentioned something he found upstairs."

Bully for him. "Oh, so he comes in, starts a row, then carries on as if it didn't happen?"

"That reminds me of you." Damon smiled.

"Don't you fucking start. I've got enough with my own self beating me up. Come on then, let's see what it is. I'm starving now, and we've still got to wait for Gilbert."

"Apparently he'll be a while."

"How do you know this?"

"Paul phoned him to see how long he'd be."

"Right. On we go then."

She followed Damon upstairs to the bathroom.

"Oh, pack it the fuck in," she said, hands on hips, staring at the white tiles that were three-deep around the bath.

Every one of them had an ear drawn on them. They weren't intricate, mainly just the squiggly outline, so it hadn't taken long to put them there, but still, to hang around in someone's house and leave them behind? And they'd ensured the front door was open so had wanted Anne found. Sara's had a key, so there was a guarantee of her being discovered by one of the men who visited—the killer must have known that. Then there was Olivia, again with the door left ajar. The person they were after knew the victims enough to know someone would be along shortly to alert the police.

Unless they had an ego the size of a barn, *why* would they want their crimes known? Most tended to conceal them, hoping they wouldn't be found, so to deliberately risk getting caught, this didn't make sense. Okay, the victims would have been found eventually, but there was an element of swiftness about this, to have the bodies discovered fast.

Someone felt the need to be noticed. Going by what was said to Sara by one of her men, that he wanted to be called a good boy, to be told 'I love you' and 'I'm proud of you'... If this was the man they were after, he was desperate for someone to care about him.

Tracy understood that more than she'd admit to anyone other than Damon and Sasha. To have had her parents behave normally... What sort of person would she have been if that had happened? Not this surly bitch, she knew that much. Maybe she'd have been the type to laugh more, to spread love all around instead of grouching and complaining, finding fault in everyone else so she didn't have to look too closely at herself.

"This case is bloody odd," Damon said.

His words drew her out of her head, somewhere she didn't usually like to be.

"It is." She studied the rest of the room. "No toothbrush. That toothpaste tube will need bagging. If it was used to clean the nails, it might have prints on it."

"Doubtful. You can bet gloves were worn."

She sighed. He was right. If the killer hadn't put them on, they were pretty stupid, but again, it pointed to them perhaps wanting to be captured. Maybe they thought they'd get the attention they craved then. To have your name down as a serial killer in the history books was a fair bit of attention, though, and life in prison could go either way—people feared you, leaving you lonely and isolated, or they made it their life's mission to make yours as uncomfortable as possible.

"Something will have been left behind," Damon said. "It's unlikely these days, what with the level of forensics, for a part of themselves not to be at a scene and us not pick it up."

"True. That'll be a matter of time then. Could be weeks before we get a hit." She wanted to kick the bath panel in frustration. Her phone bleeped, so she got it out to look at the message. "Ah, Nada's sent the photo back with the dots joined."

They bent their heads to study it.

"A maths set?" She frowned. "These pictures are so sodding random."

The items were in a row, some of the features already drawn prior to the image being completed with dots. The ruler had lines and numbers on it, the protractor and two set squares the same.

There was also an alphabet and number stencil, plus a compass and pencil.

"The compass," she said. "Used to make the dots on the bodies?"

"That fits." Damon nodded. "So does the stencil."

"Yep, one was used to write beneath the earrings at Olivia's." She sniffed. "So will the other pieces of this maths set be used at some point if there are more people on their list to kill? And how difficult must that have been to find a dot-to-dot book with this particular picture in it? I mean, really? Standing there in WHSmiths or B&M nosing at all the pages of each book until you find the one you want?"

"And…hmm, I was just going to say that was a lot of time taken to draw all the lines, letters, and numbers, but looking at the image now… We need to go to the body again."

She followed him downstairs and stood beside Anne. "What am I meant to be seeing here?"

"Don't you think that's different?" Damon pointed to Anne's midsection. "That's not the same as the other pen that was used, which we're guessing is a black Sharpie. The lines et cetera are too precise, too uniform. The ink's slightly blue. What does that remind you of?"

"Damon, I'm hungry, I'm tired. Stop fucking about and just come out with it, will you?"

"It's that carbon copy paper or something similar. The image was created previously—so premeditation—and pressed onto the skin, like they do with tattoos."

"Premeditation—that's been obvious from the bloody start, but I get what you're saying." She peered closer. "Yep, it would have taken too long for them to do this freehand, so they must have known they didn't have the time to piss-arse around here. They deliberately left the door ajar, so they could have been watching Anne for a while to know Val would be back to find her. They'd already killed Sara and Olivia so were maybe tired, too, and just needed to get the job done and leave."

"I didn't get a chance to tell you what Elsie Fordenham said."

"And I forgot to ask." Like she needed to admit to that after bawling York out earlier, for God's sake.

"It's regarding the van parked outside. A man got out of it and knocked on the door, and they chatted for a bit. He showed Anne a piece of paper—or papers, Elsie couldn't see that clearly if it was more than one—then Anne let him in."

York must have told her all this when Tracy had tuned her out. "Interesting. A white van again. Val said Anne *never* allows anyone inside. She was too afraid to because her ex was a wanker and scared the crap out of her. So she changed her behaviour for this new man, why?"

"Elsie said he seemed official, like the police. He had a uniform, including a stab vest."

"What?"

"The perfect way to gain entry, so if he isn't one of us or a person in, say, the security business, he's got that uniform and vest from somewhere."

"I'll send that info to Nada now. One of the team can have a poke around and see where those things can be bought." She did that then took a picture of the wall above the mantel. Who was the whore-slapper-bitch, and what did she have to stop? And who was the person who was angry about her behaviour when she was married and had a kid—the husband or the son?

Questions she needed the bloody answers to, and she'd get them, but first she'd have food, visit Anne's next of kin if she had any, have a meeting with her team back at the station, and hopefully, if all went well, she could go home and get some sleep, ready to begin again.

Mondays were always shit, and tomorrow would be no exception.

CHAPTER TWELVE

Mike had the day off. He didn't work Mondays so could spend it killing Peggy as many times as he could manage. Up with the advent of dawn, he showered and let Dot out for a quick wee in the back garden. She snuffled around for a few minutes while he drank his coffee and thought about Deirdre Kaggle.

She lived alone, as far as he'd worked out from watching her for a full week. He'd first seen her in Sainsbury's when he'd turned into the World Food aisle for some Nerds—he liked those, especially the long rope ones. She'd been stretching up to take a can of Mexican beans off the top shelf, on her tiptoes, grunting with the effort. He'd stopped short, breath catching, and stared, thinking Peggy had come back. His heart hadn't taken kindly to the sight of her, thumping madly, creating some sort of hollow, as though it didn't even exist, yet it had beat hard—too hard—so was there all right.

He'd walked up to her and reached for the can, and she'd faced him, her cheeks flushed, and thanked him for helping her out. He hadn't been bloody helping her out, he'd wanted to check if it was *her*, and it wasn't, but his head wasn't taking any notice of that.

"That's okay," he'd said, smiling, and it felt so wrong to do that to her, because she was Peggy in his mind, no matter that it was clear she was someone else. He'd popped the item in her basket and stared at her as she'd waddled away—she'd put on a lot of weight.

She must have sensed him doing it, because she'd turned to look over her shoulder, frowned, then scuttled off, disappearing around the corner, maybe into another aisle or perhaps to linger at the end of this one until he'd gone, feigning a study of the Schwartz spices or whatever the hell was on those shelves.

He'd realised the power he had then, where women were scared of him, and he hadn't done anything except fetch the can and smile, so it must have been the smile that had done it—and to many ladies on his list since. He'd tried it out just to see, and a lot of them had all but run away from him once he'd shown them his teeth.

It might have been the fact that he slid his tongue over them. Females probably thought he was being a pervert, licking, showing what he wanted to do to them *down there*, but that wasn't it at all. Those women brought out uncertainty in him, and that was why he did it.

He'd have to make sure he didn't lick again when he saw Deirdre. A moment of unease slithered through him at the thought of her recognising him, even with the fake moustache and the hair on his cap. She'd looked right into his eyes in Sainsbury's and might know them again, especially if he'd given her the creeps like he suspected he had.

Sod it. Too late now. She was the next one, and nothing was going to stop that.

Around nine, he told Dot he wouldn't be long and walked through the alley and garage area into Bluebird Avenue, putting his kill things in the back of his van alongside his work tools. Tomorrow he had a boiler to see to, some old dear who'd booked him in to give it a yearly gas check, and he hoped he wouldn't be too tired to do it. He didn't want to let her down.

He patted his pouch to make sure he'd remembered to attach it to his uniform trouser belt loops and, satisfied everything was in order, he got in and put the High Court writ on the passenger seat. In his disguise, the moustache tickling his nose, he drove to Deirdre's, parking in her next-door neighbour's spot, seeing as she was out at work at the lumber factory. He'd followed them all at some point so he knew what time they arrived and left their employment. Best to be prepared.

Gloves on—the black leather added a menacing touch to his uniform, he reckoned—he collected his High Court writ and approached Deirdre's door. After he gave a brisk knock, she opened up and smiled at him. He did the same in return, although he remembered not to lick his gnashers.

"Good morning," he said. "Deirdre Kaggle, isn't it?"

She looked him up and down, seeming to register his uniform for the first time. "Oh, have I done something wrong?"

She thought he was the police, and wasn't that funny? "If not paying a debt is wrong, then yes, you have. And it is wrong, isn't it? You had the money, so you should pay it back."

She frowned and reared her head a bit. "Debt?"

"I'm a High Court enforcement agent, and I'm here to collect the sum of five thousand, four hundred and fifty-one pounds. Do you have the means to pay this today, madam?"

"Of course I bloody don't! Who has that kind of cash to hand?"

He thought about the people on the TV show and how they liked to give the agents the runaround. "So are you going to mess me about for a bit, pretend you don't have the cash, then suddenly, when I enter the property—which I'm legally allowed to do—and begin making an inventory to take items from your home to the value of the debt, you'll magically find it, or think of someone who can come to your rescue with their trusty credit card?"

"No! If I haven't got it, I haven't got it. And what do you mean, enter the property? You're not fucking coming in here."

Oh, that was a bit feisty, wasn't it. "I'm afraid I am coming in if you don't pay up, Mrs Kaggle."

"It's Miss, so if that writ has Mrs on it, it's null and void. You won't be able to come in if it isn't correct."

Blimey, did she watch that TV programme, too? He'd bet she did. Otherwise, how would she know something like that? Thankfully, he'd prepared for this. "It doesn't have anything but your name on it." He held the paper up and made a show of reading it. "Yes, that's right, Deirdre Kaggle. Not many of that name about, so I assume I have the right person. Besides"—he sighed like she was some silly billy and bored him—"this is from the High Court, so I doubt very much if it's wrong."

She opened her mouth to spout some other rubbish, but he ploughed on.

"If you don't have the money, I suggest you step aside and allow me to come in. If you don't, it doesn't matter, I'll come in anyway."

"What's this debt meant to be for?" She scrunched her eyebrows.

"You had a load of aeroplane chairs and didn't send them to the buyer." That had been on one of the episodes, those chairs, and they hadn't been seized because they were a specialist item and were unlikely to sell at auction. He took notice of things like that.

She released a shitty little laugh. "Aeroplane chairs? Are you *kidding* me?"

"I don't kid, *Miss* Kaggle." He wondered whether she'd been too ugly to marry. She was well past her sell-by date so had clearly been passed over, left on the dusty shelf.

"Let me see that bloody writ." She reached out to snatch it.

Mike held it close to his chest. "If you can look at it in a less aggressive manner, I'll show you. I won't hand it over, though. You'll have to read it while I hold it up." God, she was like a monkey after a banana, that one, all grabby hands. "Are you going to behave?" It was fun to mess around with her, knowing no one else in the street was witnessing it. They were all plodding through the start of their daily grind, probably drinking tea or coffee at their desks, maybe munching on a custard cream while they were at it, crumbs dropping on their keyboards.

Deirdre nodded.

"Good." He raised the paper so she could scan the words.

A big huff. "I'm telling you, I did *not* purchase aeroplane seats," she sniped, seemingly peeved that the writ was in order.

He was proud of himself for writing all that legal jargon. "Then that's something you'll need to sort out yourself afterwards. The money has to be paid today, or goods seized to that amount, no matter what. You've stated you don't have the funds, so I'm now going to enter your property and make an inventory, just like I said."

He brushed past her, into the house, chivvying her along with him while stuffing the writ in his trouser pocket. He kicked the door shut, and she took two steps back. There was no sign of the boxer dog.

"Now hang on a minute," she said. "No need to push me about, is there? I'm going to phone the police to check if you're who you say you are, and we can get this misunderstanding sorted out."

"*This* isn't a misunderstanding." He launched a right hook at her.

His fist connected with her nose, and she went down, a sack of flabby shit, screaming. Oh dear, what a noisy ninny. He kicked her face, and while she cried and screeched, he dragged her into the kitchen.

"Shut the fuck up!"

He shoved her onto a dining chair and grabbed a fancy pink belt off the table. Arcing his arm back, he swung the leather strap at her, lashing her face again and again with the buckle end. She raised her hands to shield herself, but he'd entered No Going Back Mode and thrashed her to within an inch of her sorry life. Her screams had been loud to start with, but she whimpered now, lowering her hands as if she realised it was inevitable that he was going to kill her.

Where was the fight for survival? Where had her will to live gone? Did Peggy know she wouldn't win against him, was that it? Was she aware he'd come for her with a bellyful of anger, not raw liver, to get revenge for everything she'd done? For what she'd put him and Dad through?

Her dog suddenly banged into the glass of the back door from outside, leaping up and down, nutting it. Mike ignored it and stared into Deirdre's eyes.

"Yeah, you know, don't you?" He whipped her some more. "You know damn well you shouldn't have worn those...fucking...earrings!"

"No," she said, but it sounded more of a groan from deep in her wobbly belly.

How had Peggy put on so much weight? She'd been eating more than those bloody Mexican beans from Sainsbury's, he saw that much. Was her new fella rich and could afford more than Dad? Had he beefed her up with all the good food Mike hadn't eaten for a while once she was gone? No beans on toast for her, he'd bet. It'd be a lot of pizza, same as she'd had when he was a kid, but she hadn't been overweight in those days, so what had happened between then and now? It had to be the bloke, shovelling food in her gob.

"You're filthy. Disgusting. How can you behave like that when you're married and have a little boy? Don't we matter?" And he remembered with those words that whipping wasn't what he was meant to do. He threw the damn belt, and it hit the wall, leaving a smear of blood on the way to the floor.

"Stop," she said, an old gramophone losing its oomph.

"I haven't even fucking started yet, you slapper."

He darted to her and grabbed her neck, blood seeping down her face in rivulets from where the belt prong had ripped a chunk from her skin. It got his gloves all dirty. That wasn't on, so he squeezed, imagining she was an icing bag and he needed to get all the stuff out of her through her eyes, nostrils, ears, and her horrible mouth.

"That's it," he said. "You die now. You see who's the boss."

She didn't even reach up to pull his hands away. The belt had done all the hard work for him, leaving her spent and unable to do what it took to get him off her. Maybe she was sorry now, ready to meet her maker, who was the Devil himself, because she didn't belong in Heaven with God. Nanny had said that once: *Peggy belongs in Hell, not here with you and that lovely boy of yours, son.*

Nanny thought Mike was lovely.

Would she think so now? He didn't visit her as often as he should, and soon she'd be dead, up there in the sky, looking after the Dots until Mike could get there. And Dad, Mike didn't see him much either. Couldn't bear to see him with his second family, the one he'd started when Mike was eighteen. New wife, new kids, no place for Mike, who'd joined the army for a stint at that time, out of sight, out of mind. When he'd come out, he hadn't really bothered reconnecting, and then Dad had got ill, and Mike couldn't bear seeing him when he—

"You did that," he shouted at Peggy, tightening his grip, even though her head tilted to one side and her tongue stuck out, inflated just her like thighs, her arms, her everything. "You made Dad find someone else and shove me to one side."

He let her go and stepped back, annoyed at the blood on his white shirt sleeves. Peggy always did leave a mess wherever she went. And Mike was the biggest mess of all.

With a massive push, he shoved her off the chair and grabbed her beneath the armpits. He lugged her into the kitchen area and, with a lot of huffing and puffing, managed to heft her up and sit her in the sink—or over it anyway. Her arse was wide and covered part of the draining board. He ripped her blouse open and stared.

How the fuck could he put the dots on *there*? Her stomach had rolls like Nanny's. There was no way he was going to get her back down and lay her out, so he'd have to work with what he had. With her head leaning on the window behind her, that stupid bloated tongue still hanging, he walked to the front door, putting it on the latch, and went out to his van, checking the street while he was at it.

No one.

He took his bag out and returned to the house.

He had work to do.

The knock at the door startled Mike, and Dad jumped, too. Maybe Nanny had come back round with pudding. She'd been here earlier to drop off some dinner, saying she'd noticed they were getting thin and that Dad mustn't act all proud if he needed a bit of a handout. While she didn't have much, she was willing to share what she had.

Dad was lucky to have her as his mum.

Them being skinny now, though... That was what meals of beans on toast and maybe a fried egg on the side did for you, week after week. Dad didn't have much money now Mum wasn't there, taking her wage with her to that house with that man who didn't like kids.

Dad got up from the dining table, and the new Dot scampered around his ankles, a boy this time, but Mike had kept the same name anyway. Nanny had said, in her kindly way, that getting another dog in their circumstances was a bit silly and another mouth to feed, not to mention the cost of buying it in the first place, but Dad had said Mike needed the puppy to make him feel better, and besides, a mate had given it to him.

Life was so much better with a Dot in it.

"You stay there, son." Dad disappeared from the kitchen.

Mike's tummy rolled over, and he grabbed Dot for a cuddle.

Words floated to him, some he didn't understand.
"High Court writ..."
"Pay the full sum today, sir..."
"A loan with Peggy Redmond..."
"A loan? We didn't have a bloody loan!"

"You've defaulted on the payments, sir, and we need your half of the debt."

"I don't have any money, can barely feed my kid."

"We'll have to come in and seize goods then…"

"I'll phone for a collection van, sir."

Mike ran out of the kitchen and into the hallway. Two men stood at the front door—police?—and his heart did a somersault. He raced upstairs with Dot in his arms and hid beneath the bed, and that brought painful memories back of the times he'd done that when Mum was horrible, and the night Mum had gone out with Gabby, and God, Mike missed Gabby with her cheery smile and her calling him Scamp.

Tears burned, and Dot licked them off his cheeks.

There were footsteps, Dad saying, "No, please, God, no!"

Someone came into Mike's room, their shiny black shoes appearing beneath the edge of his dangling quilt. Mike stared at them, willing the man to go away, and he did, saying, "Nothing we can take in here."

"Decent TV in the living room," the other shouted.

"Please stop," Dad said. "Please, my boy watches his cartoons on that."

"Not our problem, sir."

"So my wife will be paying the other half, will she?"

"I can't discuss her side of the debt."

They seemed to be there for ages, nosing around, the scrapes and knocks from furniture being moved loud and ominous. By the time they'd gone, Mike had cried an ocean, and Dad was crying, too, his sobs wending their way up into Mike's ears.

Ears. Mum's. He wanted to find her and slice them off.

Eventually, he crawled out from under the bed and looked around. Everything was the same. On the landing, Dot sticking by his side, he peered into Dad's room. The small TV in there was gone. Mike went downstairs, Dot leading the way, his ears flapping, tail wafting from side to side.

Dad was in the living room, sitting on the floor. No sofa and no chairs. The TV and the cabinet were gone, and all that remained was the rug in the middle, the one Nanny had apparently bought when Mum and Dad had first got married, to help 'get them on the ladder', whatever that meant.

Well, the ladder no longer had any rungs, and Mike and Dad were stuck at the bottom with no way to climb up.

"I'm so sorry, son," Dad said.

He hugged Mike, and they sat together, Dot on Mike's lap, and they had a bit of a cry. Then Dad gave Nanny a ring, and she arrived on the doorstep so quickly afterwards, their angel, the one who told them they needed to 'leave this fucking awful place' and start again. Go to hers for a few months, save, and begin a new life.

"She's got a bloody cheek, she has, that Peggy," Nanny said. "It was a cold day in Hell when the Devil brought her into this world, but it'll be a sunny one when Karma takes her the fuck out of it, and she will."

No, not she. He. Mike was going to be Karma when he was a big boy.

Mike left Deirdre's house, his head full of memories he wished he could suppress, but they were always there, taunting him, laughing at him: *Look at you, Mr Still Stuck in the Past, having to kill your mummy again and again.*

"Fuck off," he muttered, shoving his bag in the back of the van. He got in and revved the engine, so pissed off about the state of his shirt. He'd have to go home, get showered and changed, and buy a new one. No amount of soaking in salt would get the stains out of this one. But he hadn't expected to whip the stupid cow, had he, that had just happened, so he couldn't berate himself too much. At least when killing Sara he'd put on a boiler suit before he'd done the decorating with her blood.

He'd put the black bin liner with the suit inside on the hallway floor when he'd come home. Was it still there? He couldn't remember.

As he nosed the car to the close opening, he stopped in alarm. A postal van had parked, and a man sat inside smoking, staring down at his lap. Mike checked his shirt sleeves, paranoid the bloke would see them if he glanced up. And why was the postie here anyway? There hadn't been any deliveries when he'd sat here watching the street for that week, so someone must have ordered something, and that annoyed him more than it should. But there was a good side to that. The man would see Deirdre's door open and find her sooner than Mike had planned—he'd imagined her neighbour doing it later, the lumber woman.

A silver lining then. Nanny said to always look for one.

He drove home, avoiding any CCTV, and just had to hope there weren't any hidden cameras he wasn't aware of. He parked in Bluebird, took his cap and moustache off, then reached into the back for his puffa jacket so no neighbours spotted the bloodied shirt.

He made it inside without anyone coming out to have a natter—and they did some days, asking him questions about boilers and gas in general, like his expertise was theirs for free instead of calling him and asking him to visit their houses in a work capacity. Did they think his advice wasn't worth paying for? Cheeky bastards.

He took his coat off in the hallway and hung it on the newel post. He'd have to wash it later, after he'd killed more Peggys, and besides, it only had blood on the inside, transfer from his shirt, and, he noticed to his annoyance, the pissing stab vest had some on it. That would need a good sponging.

Dot went a little mad when he opened the kitchen door. She bounded off her bed and launched herself at him. She was a big, soppy thing, and her weight propelled him backwards into the doorframe. She plonked her paws on his shoulders and licked the vest, and Mike wondered what Peggy's blood tasted like and whether Dot was enjoying it. He raised his arm to his mouth and sucked the shirt sleeve, the faint tang of blood on his tongue similar to the raw liver. That similarity soured his gut, and he gently pushed Dot down and stripped to get the disgusting stench off him.

With the shirt in the sink, water and salt covering it—didn't hurt to give it a go in getting the mess out of the material—he sponged the larger splodges of blood off the vest and his trousers, laying them on the warm rad to dry. The shower took the Peggy stench off him, and while he was in there, he thought about Rona Danridge, the next one on the list. She wasn't going to be easy. He'd seen her in action, shouting at a man in the pub for leering at her in a pervy way, stopping him from pinching her bum as he'd sidled past.

No, she'd need a different approach, no High Court enforcement agent behaviour from him. Once he'd bought a new white shirt, that would take him to just the right time she'd be coming out of the gym. If he was early, he'd wait. There were no cameras there, but his cap plus the moustache would be something to hide behind. He might even add a beard.

Karma for this job was a hairy bastard.

CHAPTER THIRTEEN

Harry was having more than a sneaky breather. He'd parked up at Roundhay Close for a ciggie to begin with. He was well ahead with his deliveries, and if someone back at the depot noticed he'd stopped and his handheld machine wasn't logging signatures, or however the hell else they knew exactly what he was doing and where, he'd say the van had played up. The thing was, he'd finished his fag and rested his head back for a minute, and the next thing, he was waking up to the sound of his phone blaring out *Bohemian Rhapsody*.

Shit. If it was who he suspected, there'd be thunder and lightning, very, very frightening in his future if he didn't pull this off.

"Hello, mate," he said to the bloke back at the depot, even though he wasn't a mate and never would be.

It was Vincent, a posh bastard who spoke with more than just a plum in his mouth. He had the whole bleedin' tree, or did they grow on bushes?

Harry slapped the side of his head to get himself to concentrate.

"Where are you?" Vincent said, the hoity-toity prick, and he'd probably know where Harry was anyway.

"Roundhay Close." Harry made himself sound weary, like he'd been right through the mill. "Bloody van carked it on me, didn't it, but it's all right now. I had a fiddle with the spark plugs—my old man taught me how to do that. Worked a treat. Just about to get on with the rest of the deliveries now."

"You should be back here already," Vincent admonished.

And you should piss off. "I know. Can't be helped. Shouldn't be too long, so don't get your boxers in a wad. I've only got this parcel and one other to do."

"I don't wear boxers, I go commando."

TMI or what. "Didn't need to know that."

"But now you do. Hurry up. You need to reload."

If I had a gun, I'd reload it and shoot your brains out.

Harry thought stuff like that far too often. His mates reckoned he needed help, but he'd read somewhere that everyone thought stuff like that from time to time, and it didn't mean they needed therapy. Sod that for a game of soldiers, as his grandad was fond of saying. What that meant, Harry had no idea, but it sounded good, so he said it a lot.

"Yep, will do." He ended the call and shoved his phone in his pocket.

Vincent could knob off and do one. Harry would take as long as he liked.

He drove to number three where Deirdre Kaggle lived, the fat old bird who always insisted on sending him away with a cup of tea in one of those paper to-go cups. She was a good sort, but a bit weird, and if she offered him an orange or mint Club today, he'd love her forever. He liked those biscuits, could eat a whole packet in one sitting if Mum wasn't there to keep an eye on his scoffing. Trouble was, Deirdre had been giving him Trio bars lately, and they just weren't the same.

He parked and steeled himself for a boatload of convo. She liked to talk, Deirdre did, and her chatter would suit him fine today, seeing as Vincent would be foaming at the mouth if Harry arrived even later.

Chuckling, he got out of the van and collected the parcel from the back. The weight and feel of it was like a set of drinking glasses or something. He liked guessing what the boxes contained. Saved him going mental through boredom. Once, he'd imagined Mr Benson in Heron Road had ordered a dildo for his skinny bumhole. Turned out it was a slim vase his wife had bought—Mr Benson had said so the next time Harry had delivered there. Probably because Harry had joked the previous package had been long and slender, and what are you going to get up to with that, Mr Benson, you saucy devil?

He laughed at himself and walked up Deirdre's path. The door was ajar, so she must have come out earlier when he was napping and forgot to close it again. He hoped she didn't phone the depot and grass him up, especially now he'd lied to Vincent.

"Miss Kaggle?" he called, the package getting a bit heavy. Must be crystal tumblers, the sort you used for whiskey. "Hellooooooo! A parcel for you." He rapped on one of the glass panels.

He didn't know what to do. It wasn't like he could just waltz inside, was it. He didn't need a signature, so he could pop it on the floor and be done with it. All the neighbours were usually out, so he couldn't leave it with them. And anyway, he wanted tea and a biscuit, which meant he'd risk it and push the door wider. It eased back slowly, revealing the laminate-floored hallway and the stairs to the left. Ahead was the kitchen and—

"Oh, fuck me!" He almost dropped the parcel but managed to keep a grip on it, albeit at an awkward angle, one of the sharp corners digging into his groin. He raised it to his stomach and blinked.

Deirdre sat on the sink, her belly and tits hanging out. As if that grim sight wasn't enough, she had a face full of blood, and her tongue was...

"Sod this for a game of soldiers," he said and backed down the path, then turned and jogged to his van. Inside, her parcel dumped on the passenger seat, he got his phone out and rang the police, thinking about that orange Club and cuppa he wasn't going to get now.

Bloody hell!

CHAPTER FOURTEEN

"Miss Dandridge, would you mind having a little chat for a minute?"

Rona turned to the front desk in the gym lobby, her stomach churning, and smiled at today's receptionist, Toni Morin, who was bound to ask about the direct debit for her membership not being paid the other day. Some prat had had a whale of a time using Rona's bank details to have a shopping spree online, the night before her gym money had been due out. The bank had since put a stop on her card and reimbursed her, but she hadn't got around to letting people know what was going on.

"Is it about my subscription payment?" Rona then went on to explain what had happened, hoping Toni wouldn't be a jobsworth and start spouting contract bullet points.

"Ah, in that case, you can pay by card now, if you like," Toni said.

"I can't. I'm waiting for a new one." This was so awkward, and Rona cursed herself for even coming today when it was Toni's stint on the desk—the other receptionist hadn't bothered her.

I should have waited until the mess was fully sorted before coming here.

"A credit card then?" Toni smiled.

"Um, I don't have one of those." Heat burned Rona's cheeks. Why did life have to be so difficult? She had so much pressure lately, and she'd told herself last night to jack it all in and move elsewhere, but running wouldn't solve her problems, so she'd have to stay put and ride this out.

Toni tucked a strand of hair behind her ear. "As you know, your subscription is thirty pounds per month, and if your bank declines a payment, you have to pay for the individual sessions you've had here since the decline. It's in your contract—small print, but there all the same." She looked at her watch, scribbled something on a pad, then tapped at her keyboard with her long, black-tipped nails. "Each session costs six pounds if you're not on a contract, and it says here you've had five so…" She glanced up and smiled.

Rona couldn't believe this. What a rip-off. "So you want sixty quid instead of the original thirty?"

"That's right." Toni's smile was now a beam and a half, but it didn't look as though she was grinning from enjoyment, more like she had no choice but to do her job and present a cheery face to the customers whether she was spouting shit or not.

"I haven't got that much cash on me, or in my bank, so you'll just have to swivel." Rona shouldn't have been so rude, but for God's sake, how much more could she cope with? "I won't come here until the subscription's been paid, and if the owner still thinks I need to cough up for the five sessions, I'll just cancel my membership and go elsewhere."

Tina pressed a few keys. "Yes, I see you're at the point where you can cancel without getting penalised, but if I could just ask you to reconsider going elsewhere…?"

"I'm not staying where I'm expected to pay twice in one month when it wasn't my fault. Christ." The gym was Rona's only pleasure, the one thing she spent on herself each month apart from a glass of wine once a week at the pub, maybe a takeaway if she was lucky. The rest of her wages went into her flat and food, plus she'd had to skint herself by taking out a loan for her sister who'd fucked up and owed a shedload of rent arrears. Said sister couldn't afford the repayments like she'd promised, so Rona was stuck with them until they could work something out.

"If you stay with us, we could waiver the thirty pounds for the five sessions," Tina said.

Rona wanted to scream. Blood pulsed in her temples from anger that swept through her in a mad wave. "You *what*? So basically, this whole conversation was pointless, because now you're saying I *don't have to pay for those five days*? I give up!"

She stomped across the foyer, pissed off at having her time wasted. Six years she'd been at this gym, and not once had she defaulted on a payment, and this was the way they treated her? Fuck them. She may as well go to the sports centre instead. She'd heard that for the same price, she could also use the swimming pool, sauna, and all the evening activity classes, like yoga and whatnot.

Outside, she got her phone out and accessed her bank app, where she cancelled the gym direct debit. They'd send her a letter about the default, and she'd pay that, but anything else, they could stuff it up their arses. She wasn't made of money. While she walked, she put up a quick rant on Facebook, telling her friends what had just happened, adding a rage-face emoji for good measure, plus a knife one—yes, she felt murderous right now and had done for a while. When life spiralled out of control, you tended to go a bit off the rails, didn't you.

Automatically rounding the corner to the car park, head bent, she answered a comment that had gone up.

Rona Dandridge: **Charlotte X** Thanks, I agree. I'm definitely going to the sports centre.

Phil with the Skill: I've told you before to use the gym in my garage. We can have a different kind of session afterwards as well. [WINK EMOJI]

Rona Dandridge: **Phil with the Skill** Knob off, will you! I'm not in the mood.

Phil with the Skill: Shame, you never are. You don't know what you're missing. And speaking of knobs…

Rona dropped her phone in her bag, not in the right frame of mind to deal with Phil, who was a right perv but didn't mean anything by it. He liked to mess around with girls, and she reckoned if any of them took him up on his offers, he'd run a mile. She'd bet he wouldn't even know what to do with his dick anyway.

And today couldn't get any worse. Some weirdo bloke stood between her car and his van, bending over and fiddling with the key in his passenger-side door. Long hair draped from beneath a baseball cap, and she reckoned rats could live in that beard it was so long and unkempt. He glanced her way and smiled, his teeth breaking up all that fuzziness. With him there, he was blocking her driver's door, so she'd have to wait for him to stop fucking about before she could get in. She was due at work by twelve and had yet to have a shower. Toni had held her up long enough as it was.

"Excuse me, but can I just get into my car, please?" she said, waiting by her back bumper.

He pressed his arse to the rear side of his van, and she wasn't comfortable with walking past him, so close, but she'd just have to get over it. Time really wasn't her best friend this morning. So she turned, facing her car, and stepped sideways, sensing his crotch by the top of her bum as she ventured along. She fumbled for her key in her bag, then managed to slide it in the lock, her hand shaking, legs going weak. This felt too intimate, too out of her comfort zone, and the quicker she got in, the better. Her earlier anger had switched to fear, and the adrenaline from both left her queasy.

She pulled the door open, then a massive pain speared through her head from behind, and she nutted the roof of the car. She instinctively reached up to press the back of her skull. A palm slapped across her mouth, her bum jabbing into his...his groin. There was no chance for her to get a scream out, and then hands were around her neck, choking, squeezing so hard stars danced in front of her.

"You filthy, open-your-legs slag, Peggy," he said.

Oh God, he sounded like that freak in the Chinese takeaway the other night, the one who'd asked her if she fancied going out on a date, and he'd licked his teeth, giving her the creeps. But it couldn't be him, he hadn't had a beard or hair, he was bald, and anyway, she wasn't Peggy, so he'd got the wrong woman. How could she tell him, though, when he was—*oh my God, oh my God, he's killing me!*

Rona tried lifting her hands ready to grab his wrists, but her arms were too heavy. She panicked and kicked backwards, only meeting air. Her lungs strained through lack of oxygen, and the pain in her throat was immense. Darkness crept in from the edges of her vision, slinking over the sight of the steering wheel to the right, her seat to the left, and finally bleeding in towards her gearstick.

Then nothing but black, the sound of her gurgling, the tightness of her burning lungs, and him saying, "You're going to regret stabbing the Dots with that compass, you hateful bitch, just you wait and see."

Dots? Compass?

Rona's mind shut down, and she sank into nothingness.

She came to with the biggest headache she'd ever had and a dry tongue that stuck to the roof of her mouth. She couldn't open her eyes; they seemed stuck down, weighted with sleep. She'd lie here for a bit before she got up to go to the gym and then—

The gym. Toni giving her all that guff about paying sixty quid. Was that yesterday?

She frowned, trying to work it out. She'd left the gym, and that man had been by her car, and—

That man. Long hair. Beard. The whack to her head.

Her heart rate scattered, and she snapped her eyes open, glancing around in panic. Her head throbbed from the movement, and she winced, not recognising her surroundings at all. A bedroom. White wallpaper with flowers. Pink curtains. She turned onto her side on top of a single bed and faced a dark set of wooden drawers and a matching wardrobe with a full-length mirror on one of the doors. She stared at herself. It wasn't her tongue stuck to the roof of her mouth but a ball of fabric, and a gag had been tied tight, a strip of weird Aztec material between her lips.

Where was her bag? She looked around for it, but it wasn't there. She needed to find it so she could get her phone and call for help.

Panic set in. She recalled what the man had said. He thought she was someone called Peggy, and he must have brought her here in his van. Where was here? How long had she been out of it? Was it still today, or had time passed so much that someone would be wondering where she was?

A flicker of movement, then he stood there in the doorframe, a knife in one hand.

"You're awake," he said.

She went to speak but remembered the gag.

"I wasn't going to bring you here, Peggy, but decided I need answers. I want a proper conversation, where you tell me just what you were thinking back then, and why you did what you did." He took a step inside. "I can barely stand to fucking look at you, so it's going to be difficult, but you *will* explain things to me, and you *will* say you're sorry before I—"

Before he what? *What?*

Her skin went cold, and she shivered from fear. If she got up and rushed at him, she could knock him flying and get out of here. Her wrists and ankles weren't bound, so she wasn't restricted, but that knife put her off.

"Come with me," he said and moved forward, grabbing the top of her arm. He yanked her up on her feet and pushed her in the back. "Go downstairs. Don't even think about running out, the front and back doors are locked."

She stumbled onto the landing then took the stairs slowly, her head spinning, insistent throbs at the top of her neck matching her heartbeat. In the hallway, she eyed the front door—a chain and two bolts; she wouldn't have time to fiddle with them.

"The kitchen," he snapped.

Rona wandered along and entered through the doorway at the end. She stopped at the sight of a whiteboard on a tripod. It had dots all over it—dots…hadn't he mentioned that by her car?—and numbers and…and…she couldn't make out what the drawing was. Maybe a handle, plus some wheels?

"Sit," he said. "We'll be civilised at the table, but if it turns to shit, our chat, then I'll stop forcing myself to be nice and treat you like the other Peggys."

She shuddered and walked forward, the floor cold on her feet. He'd taken her trainers off while she'd slept? The idea of him having access to every part of her and she hadn't known it… A wave of sickness swept up her windpipe, and she swallowed down bile.

"Go on, slowcoach. Sit."

She took another pace forward and screeched at the sharp agony searing her foot. A glance down told her why. Glass shards littered the tiles.

"Hurt, does it?" he said right by her ear, his breath hot and smelly. "Now you know how little Dot felt." He pinched her earlobe. "Now. Fucking. Sit. Down!"

She choked on a sob and limped over to do as he'd said, scoping out the back door. Two more bolts and a key in the lock. Daylight seeped around the blind over the glass and the one at the window above the sink. The wooden chair was hard beneath her bum, her back to the rear door, the whiteboard to her left, and she still shivered, unable to stop herself. He sat opposite, his eyes piercing, his lips two flat lines inside the beard. He reached up, and she flinched in case he smacked her one, but he took his cap off, his straggly hair coming away with it.

What?

She frowned at his bald head.

He picked at the top of his beard by his temple and peeled it downwards, revealing a face she knew, and she inhaled through her nose in shock. The man in the Chinese.

"I see you know who I am, Peggy. I'm surprised you even remember. So many years have passed." He dropped the beard on top of the cap on the table and placed the knife down.

Years? It was only last week, for fuck's sake. The extreme urge to get up and attack him came over her, but fear kept her rooted to the seat. She glanced at the knife, then back to him. His eyes, they were terrible, full of hatred, and narrowed, like he thought she was a piece of shit.

"I'm going to join the dots, and you're going to explain the picture it makes." He got up and moved to the whiteboard. Picked up a thick black marker. Stood side-on while he worked, probably so he could keep her in his sights. He must have sensed her intention—he grabbed the knife and slid it in his pocket, the end of the blade poking out. It had two points.

He returned to his task. The marker squeaked every so often, the sound hurting her sore head. She glanced at the kitchen door, the one she'd come through, and worked out whether it was worth her darting out, shutting it to buy time, then doing her best to open the front door.

"I wouldn't if I were you, slut," he said. "He isn't here to save you now. Your new man isn't waiting in his car like he was on the night you left. Did he bring you back early in the morning to stab Dot with my compass after she'd been let out for a wee?"

Who was he on about? She didn't have a new man—hadn't had a boyfriend in over a year—and as for this Dot, she was clueless. And who stabbed people with a compass?

"Now then. Tell me all about this." He tapped the whiteboard with the marker, then placed it on the little silver ledge at the bottom.

She stared at the marker. If she was fast enough, she could grab it and ram it in his eye.

"Tell me!" he shouted, leaning towards her, his face going red and spittle flying.

Fucking hell, fucking hell…
She pointed to her mouth.
"For Pete's sake." He shoved a pad and pencil at her across the table. "Write it down, you dumb cow."
She lifted the pencil.

I don't know who you think I am, but I'm not Peggy. I don't have a boyfriend, and I have no clue who Dot is. As for the picture you drew, it's just a suitcase. What am I supposed to be seeing?

He slapped her across the face, and her cheek stung, eyes watering. "You absolute bitch. You know exactly who you and Dot are, who *all* the Dots are, and if you don't have a boyfriend, why did you tell Dad you were leaving him for another man?"
She blinked away tears brought on by the slap and swallowed.
He was mad, had to be.

I don't know who your dad is. I've never seen you before in my life until you asked me out in the Chinese, so how can I know him?

He growled. "So you're pretending now, is that it? Making out you don't know us? Is that how you sleep at night? Is that how you justify it all?" He grabbed a fistful of her hair and lowered his face to hers.

She raised the pencil, ready to attack with it, and he bit the end of her nose then released her with such force the chair scooted back.

"Don't you fucking dare try hurting me more than you already have," he snarled. "Answer my questions."

She didn't write anything.

"Well, *is it*? Is that how you justify it?" he roared. "You'd better fucking answer me, woman, or so help me, I'll kill you all over again."

Rona froze at that. Kill again? So he'd killed this Peggy before? If he had, why the hell did he think she was her? He was bloody mental!

I don't understand. I swear, I'm not Peggy. My name is Rona Danridge, and I've never been married. The suitcase means nothing to me except you use one to go on holiday. You've mixed me up with someone else— <u>PLEASE BELIEVE ME!</u>

"Believe you?" He laughed. "Why should I? You've lied to me all my life, and when I grew up and saw you again, I made sure you remembered who I am. You pissed yourself, remember that?"

It was getting harder to keep hold of the pencil. Sweat coated her palms and fingers, and if he shouted at her for much longer, she'd shake so badly she wouldn't be able to write. *Then* what would he do?

"Right, that's it. You had your chance." He snatched the pad away, throwing it across the room. "I'm going to take you home."

Her heart flickered with wild beats, and relief surged through her. Then panic returned. What if he took her to this Peggy woman's house?

"Nineteen Pelican Place," he muttered, scooping up her bag from the corner and hanging it over his shoulder.

So he knows where I live. How? Has he been following me? Watching me?

Fear pelted through her, and oddly, she was glad of him wrenching her to her feet—she wouldn't manage it by herself. The motion had her dropping the pencil, though. Adrenaline flushed her system to such a degree she seemed too heavy to move. His gloved fingertips dug into her muscles, and she clenched her teeth, some of the material in her mouth wedged between the molars on one side.

"We'll go out the back way," he said. "Out through my gate, past the trees, and straight into the car park then into Bluebird, got it? No deviating. If you do, I'll kill you there and then and fuck the consequences."

She hobbled, trying not to put pressure on the foot with the glass in it.

"Be back later, Dot," he called.

So this Dot person was here, too? Maybe in the living room? She had no time to think about it any longer. He opened the door and pushed her outside. She'd do exactly what he said until there was a time she could get away.

But that plan was dashed when he gripped the back of her neck and steered her down the garden path, waving the knife. She wouldn't be trying to escape now, and he knew it.

"Fuck me about, and I'll slit your throat, right?"

She nodded, letting the tears fall, the snot dribble, the sobs suffocate her.

"And shut the hell up, you dirty tart, you're getting on my wick."

She thought about her chat with Toni. If she hadn't had it, this nutter might not have been at her car when Rona had gone outside. The same if she'd stayed in the gym for a bit longer.

Loan repayments and a thief using her debit card suddenly didn't seem so important anymore. Staying alive was.

CHAPTER FIFTEEN

Tracy shook her head. Monday was going to be just as shit as Sunday. She'd been pulled from her paperwork in her office to come out to this scene, and going by what she'd heard so far, the killer had struck again.

Harry Yew, a postman, had just recited his version of events, sounding more chagrined about a biscuit and a cup of tea than the actual murder. People were weird. She was annoyed with him, although it wasn't really his fault, but if he'd looked up after parking instead of smoking and gawping at his phone, he'd have seen the killer leaving, but all they had to go on was that he vaguely recalled a vehicle driving out of the turning—he'd only seen it in his peripheral, so that wasn't any help. He didn't remember a colour or whether it was a van.

"Can I go now?" he asked. "Vincent is going to go mad when I get back, and I still need to drop off the last package."

"Who is Vincent?"

"My line manager. I told you, he rang me."

"You did, yes, but you never mentioned his name."

A SOCO had relieved Harry of Deirdre's parcel and was currently opening it in the back of the SOCO van inside a large plastic box so any evidence would fall in there. While they'd usually have it taken to the lab, they needed to know what was inside it. Whatever it was might relate to the case, and spending time waiting for the lab to get back to them could put them behind in the investigation.

As if we're not behind enough already.

She'd already checked the post van, and one package remained. "Yes, you can go. We have your details, and you'll need to give a full statement at some point. We'll be in touch. If you remember anything in the meantime, ring me." She handed him her card.

He got in his van and drove away, and Tracy waved at Gilbert who'd just pulled up. He must have finished at the two previous scenes. Paul Dunnings was inside the victim's house, and a few SOCO were doing fingertip searches in the surrounding area outside.

While Gilbert put his protective suit on, Tracy walked to the SOCO van.

"What's in the parcel?" she asked.

The officer held up two glass balls. "Paperweights from an online shop called Glass Beauties. There's an invoice inside, and the deceased purchased them. It has her details on it."

"Okay, thanks." She went back to Damon and told him. "So the killer didn't order those to bash her head in with then."

"Thank God. That would have been a bit of a mess."

"More than a bit."

Gilbert ducked beneath the tape that a uniform had strung up, coming to join them. "This is giving me more exercise than I'd like, farting about from one body to the next. Still, it's keeping Kathy busy and out of our faces."

Tracy smiled. "Good."

"I didn't think you'd mind." Gilbert glanced around. "Quiet little close. No cars. I take it everyone's out bar the victim?"

"Yep. Tim's with Erica, talking to them all at work. Hopefully someone noticed a vehicle, specifically a white van, someone in it checking the street out. We might get lucky and bag a nosy one who took down the number plate."

"You're asking for a miracle," Damon said.

"I know. Nada said she's put Lara on the white van trail as well as five uniforms. They're out asking for alibis."

Gilbert cleared his throat. "You'll find who it is eventually. Someone has been busy, perhaps killing on a streak of adrenaline to fit them all in so fast."

"Or it could be two people," Damon suggested.

"Lovely." Tracy rolled her shoulders to ease the tension in her neck. "I suppose we'd better go inside and see what's going on."

Tracy and Damon suited up at the back of the SOCO van, minus the booties, which they put on in Deirdre's hallway. Log signed, they all trooped ahead to the kitchen. Paul Dunnings was there, measuring a scuff of blood to the right on the dining area wall.

Tracy stared at Deirdre Kaggle and shook her head. "Who puts a woman on a sink?"

Damon shrugged. "No idea, but it's certainly unique."

"More to the point, I think she's been whipped." Gilbert sighed.

"With a belt," Paul said. "It's over here. Blood on it, plus what appears to be a chunk of flesh on the buckle prong."

"Fuck me." Tracy clocked exactly where that flesh had come from. Deirdre's cheek. "The earlobes and eyebrows are… Hang on a bloody minute…" She peered closer. Sewing pins had been pushed through the cut-off lobes and into the eyes, and one each held the eyebrows beneath the nose.

It appeared they'd gone right into the gum, so that would take force if a tooth root was behind them. She could only hope that had been done after death. "This fucker is creative. She's sitting up, and the lobes and eyebrows would fall off, so they've made sure they don't."

"Like at Olivia's," Damon said, "although pins are preferable to the staple gun."

"Why lop off her hair and tuck it in her bra?" she asked. "It looks like spaniel ears."

"God knows."

"She has a broken nose." Gilbert stepped closer. "It's leaning to our left, so a right-handed punch or strike. Strangulation marks on the neck beneath that blood. You can see the thumbprint bruises."

"She's got a dot-to-dot on her stomach." Tracy blew out air, and it hit the inside of her face mask. Nasty and clammy.

"I'd suggest getting her down and laying her out," Gilbert said, "to see if it's on all of her stomach, because by her position, we can't see."

Deirdre's tummy had folded into two big lips. Nothing unusual there, most people's bellies did similar if you were slumped like that, but Gilbert had a point.

"Let me see if Nada can make a picture from just this bit. Then we'll know if it's complete without having to disturb Deirdre for now."

"Yes, I don't want her moved yet," Paul said.

Tracy took a photo and send it to Nada, asking her to join the dots immediately. She studied the dots. Whatever it was, was long and slim, and a narrow rectangle had been drawn halfway along.

"I'll just do the temp."

Gilbert got on with that, and Tracy moved back to give him room.

"So we have another difference," she said, "like all the others had. This time we have a thrashing with a belt and a broken nose, so rage played a part here and she was beaten up."

"There's blood on the table," Paul called out. "I suspect she was sitting and the whipping took place there."

Tracy ignored him and walked over. Small droplets, but visible as the table was white. "So do you think she was killed before being put on the sink, *Damon*?" She'd emphasised that so Paul didn't think she was speaking to him. Maybe one day she'd get over her childish self, but for now, it was still there, that need to always make a point.

"Probably."

"I'd say so," Gilbert said, "going by the marks on her neck. They're not meshing with someone strangling her in this position. She was lower. You can tell by the thumb marks. If she was here on the sink, there would be more pressure at the bottom of the thumbs, so darker bruising there. She has it at the top, so she was seated, and the killer stood over her."

"And the whipping came first, yes?" she asked.

"Yes, too much blood present," Gilbert answered. "It flowed freely down her face. Mind you, it could have been done immediately after death and created the same effect, but I'll go with beforehand." He checked the temp device. "This was pretty recent, her death. Within the last two hours."

Tracy shut her eyes for a moment. So bloody close. The killer had not long been here. Alastair was looking at CCTV of the area now, but she doubted they'd get anything from that. The killer had bypassed all cameras so far, so they'd done their homework. This had all been planned, wasn't some random spree, so they were dealing with someone who'd been meticulous in their observations of the victims prior to killing them.

Hence knowing this little street would only have Deirdre in it today.

Her phone blipped, and she checked the message.

Nada: THE PICTURE IS OF A KNIFE WITH TWO POINTED BITS AT THE END ON A CURVE. I'VE LOOKED IT UP—ITS ONE USED FOR CHEESE. THE RECTANGLE IN THE MIDDLE IS THE HILT.

Tracy: OKAY. NO INDICATION A KNIFE WAS USED WITH ANY OF THE VICTIMS YET, SO GOD KNOWS WHAT THAT'S ABOUT.

Nada: SAME WITH THE OTHER IMAGES, THOUGH. THE OCTOPUS, HOUSE, MATHS SET, AND NOW THIS KNIFE. NONE OF THEM MAKE ANY SENSE APART FROM PERHAPS THE COMPASS BEING USED TO CREATE THE DOTS.

Tracy: TRUE. WE'LL WORK IT OUT.

She jumped as a dog's face appeared behind the glass of the back door, a brown boxer with a white patch on his forehead. "Anyone sorted for that dog to be rehomed?"

Earlier, as Tracy had pulled up in the close, Nada had reported that Deirdre had no living relatives left, so it would be a job for the RSPCA or the local dogs' home.

"Yes," Paul said. "I'm taking him if there's no claim from a family member."

Oh. Tracy hadn't expected that. He might have lecherous tendencies with the way he'd ogled her when they'd first met, but he had to be a kind bloke if he was willing to foster a dead woman's dog. Then again, bastards also liked dogs, so that didn't mean anything.

"He's yours then," she said. "Deirdre had no one."

Paul walked over to the door. The dog gazed at him in adoration. Tracy looked away. The stupid, sentimental scene was going to set her off. Why was it she could witness dead bodies and accept it as par for the course, but the minute she knew this dog here wouldn't be spending time in a lonely kennel, she wanted to cry?

Fuck's sake.

"I'll call him Ali," Paul said. "You know, because he's a boxer."

"Um, whatever you like," she said. "Better than Lucky. Or are they both as clichéd as each other?"

"Probably," Paul said, "but your sour way of viewing things isn't going to taint the fact that I have a new dog to keep me company after my old one died two weeks ago, plus, Ali here has an owner who will spoil him rotten."

Well, that put her in her place, didn't it.

"You know I'm a bitch, don't you?" she asked.

"So I've heard, but there's being a bitch at appropriate times, then being one for the sake of it. This is the latter. Sometimes, keeping your mouth shut is the best option. Maybe you can learn from this, but somehow, I doubt it." He stalked out of the kitchen.

Tasting her own medicine didn't feel good. She dished out acerbic comments like Paul had all the time, and being on the receiving end oddly had her wanting to run and hide. Then she consoled herself with the fact that Paul had probably only had a pop to get back at her for sniping at him regarding his views on some criminals being placed in a hospital rather than prison.

She was good at justifying her actions.

Doesn't mean they're right, though.

Damon came over and quickly squeezed her hand, then moved away to inspect the blood on the wall.

She followed him. "I know, I shouldn't have been so cruel," she admitted. But she was damned if she'd go and find Paul to say sorry. Something in her wouldn't allow it. She'd have to talk about this with Sasha Barrows, see if the therapist could teach her how to eat humble pie. For the moment, she wasn't hungry enough to put a spoonful in her mouth, though, and that was another problem. She didn't care beyond the initial pinch of embarrassment. But her skin, while thick, had been pricked, and that was unusual.

"You are who you are," Gilbert said. "We're used to it and accept you. Mr Dunnings will have to do the same."

'Have to'. Sasha would say Paul *shouldn't* have to, that *none* of her colleagues should have to deal with her spiteful words, and she'd be right. Annoyed, and at the same time confused by this turn of events, as it had allowed questions to form that she didn't want to answer—or face—Tracy snapped out of vulnerable mode and into work at the sound of her message tone bleeping.

Nada: LOOK AT *THE HERALD*.

"Oh, for fuck's sake." Tracy took her phone out and accessed the news site.

MURDER IS RIFE YET AGAIN!

ANDY BABBITT – CRIME REPORTER

The bodies of three women were found in their homes on Sunday. Sara Scott, Olivia Zola, and Anne Walton had all been strangled, although, according to a police source, strangulation is just one of the disturbing traits of this serial killer case.

The police presence at all three locations has stirred up fear in the streets where the women lived. One neighbour, Frankie Bollen, told us how he'd found Olivia Zola after her front door was left open. Similarly, Val Edmunton found her neighbour, Anne Walton, for the same reason. Does the murderer want the bodies discovered? It would seem so, but Sara Scott's door had been closed. However, her boyfriend went inside early on Sunday morning and had the shock of seeing her dead.

At present, there are no leads for DI Tracy Collier, so let's hope she finds something soon. As is usually the way with her, too many people lose their lives prior to her finding the killer. That begs the question: Is she the right person for the job? Or should someone more competent take over?

DI Bethany Smith from Shadwell has the same issue, as does DI Helena Stratton in Smaltern—many deaths before apprehension and arrest. What are they teaching detectives these days? It certainly isn't how to capture someone who has a mind to snuff out lives. Do the investigative teams sit there eating doughnuts and drinking tea while someone has a whale of a time committing these hideous crimes?

Or it is because the SIOs are women? Controversial…

Let's try to solve this ourselves, as a community. Have you noticed anyone acting oddly over the weekend? Furtive, perhaps, or maybe they came home with blood on them. That would certainly be the case with Sara Scott, who'd had her arm slit, her blood drained, and then that blood was splashed all over the walls.

There's a madman out there. We need to find him. Ring the police station with any information you have so this person is caught—*before* any more women end up dead.

"You absolute fucking tosser," Tracy said. "Look at this shit, Damon."

He came over, and she handed him her phone. While he read, she watched Ali in the garden. The silly sod was throwing his own ball then running off to catch it. He bounded back up the garden and went on his hind legs at the door again, peering in.

"Okay, the attack on female SIOs is nasty. He's having a dig, but that's usual for Babbitt." Damon gave her phone back.

"Yeah, well, two digs at me in one day is a bit much."

"Now you know how it feels," he said, giving her shoulder a pat.

No one else would have got away with saying that.

"I do. That'll teach me."

She replied to Nada: THANKS FOR THE WARNING. WONDER WHERE HE'S GETTING HIS INFO FROM? ANY NEWS ON THE VAN OWNERS?

Nada: IGNORE HIM, THE BLOODY PRAT. AS FOR THE VANS, THERE ARE OVER A THOUSAND, SO I'LL LET YOU WORK OUT HOW LONG THAT'S GOING TO TAKE.

Tracy: WE'RE PROBABLY TALKING A MAN HERE, SO GET FEMALE ALIBIS VIA THE PHONE. TELL THOSE OUT IN THE FIELD TO CONCENTRATE ON THE BLOKES, AND ANY WITH LONGER HAIR, PLUS FACIAL, QUESTION THEM MORE DEEPLY.

Nada: OKAY.

"Right," Tracy said. "That article has really got my back up, so we need to get our skates on with this mess."

"Are you sure it's just the article?" Damon said.

"Do you even need to ask? You know Paul bugged me shitless as well. I can't talk about that, by the way. It's got me feeling things I don't want to feel."

He nodded, clearly understanding her complexities, as always. "When do you next see Sasha?"

"It isn't until next month, but I'll see if she's got a slot later. I'll pick up a takeaway afterwards. Sod cooking after a session with her. She knackers me out. All that thinking and trying to come up with ways to better myself." She rolled her eyes.

"Chinese or Indian?" he asked.

"Let's go for a disgusting kebab. I like the sauerkraut they put on it."

"That's the crappiest excuse I've ever heard."

She smiled. "Okay, the red pickled cabbage as well."

They laughed and turned to Gilbert, Tracy ready to ask him a question, when Paul shouted her from another part of the house.

She went and found him upstairs in the spare room. He was on his hands and knees, looking under the single bed. A flash came from beneath it, and she spotted the curved back of the photographer on the other side, so something of significance was there.

"That'll do," Paul said.

The photographer got up and left, so Tracy stepped inside. Paul pulled a piece of paper out with tweezers, and she stared down at it. A hand drawing of a bed, a little boy and dog hiding under it. Along the bottom, the words: LOOK WHERE I ALWAYS WENT WHEN YOU UPSET ME, YOU NASTY BITCH!

"Okay then..." Tracy snapped a copy of it with her phone.

It was a man they were searching for, no question, and she assumed he'd been a boy who'd felt the need to hide from a female. Mother? Sister? Aunt, gran, friend?

This was pointing to an individual who'd failed to let go of the past.

I know how that feels.

CHAPTER SIXTEEN

Peggy sat on the edge of her bed, crying, and it was getting right on Mike's nerves. What was the point in sobbing now, when the damage was done? And as for making out she wasn't even his mother, that was just ridiculous. She was Mum all right, with her long hair and defiant expression. Yeah, she looked pissed off even though she was blarting. Maybe it was because he'd called her ugly just now. Fugly, to be more precise.

"Why don't you just shut up?" He took her bag off his shoulder and dumped it on the floor.

She mumbled, the gag preventing him from hearing what she'd said.

"What was that?" He kicked the side of her calf. "Fucking cow."

He pushed her. Back flat on the mattress, she stared up at him, eyes wide, and lifted her hands to ward him off. He batted them away and straddled her, pressing her arms to her flanks, the sides of his knees pinning them.

"You don't get to scratch me," he said. "But I'll still pinch your toothbrush. I need it, have to keep it, and you'd never understand why. You wouldn't even care."

She said something muffled again, and he clasped her throat, lightly, giving her an inkling of what he was about to do but not quite fulfilling her expectation. He wanted the fear to linger, like it had for him during his times under the bed, then she'd know how he'd felt. Scared, helpless, and alone. And although he was with her now, she *was* alone in that she experienced feelings of having no one to help her, just like him.

But you had Dad and Nanny.

"Not under the bed I didn't, I only had Dot."

She blinked, staring as if he'd said something. Was she hearing things in her delirium? He liked the idea of that. *He'd* heard things, too, while hiding—the creak of the stairs, as if some monster was coming up them; the scrape of a skeletal tree branch sliding across the window in the wind; the cackle of Peggy's laughter, even though she wasn't there. *She wasn't fucking there!* And that was the reason for all this, her absence, her lack of caring that she'd left him with Dad, and even though he'd been glad at the time that he'd never have to see her again after she'd gone to be with that man, it still hurt. Her rejection of him. Her saying she didn't give a shit about him or Dad.

So much pain.

He tightened his hold on her neck a little and closed his eyes, running his tongue over his teeth to calm him, stop him doing this too soon. She needed to suffer while he drew it out. She needed to understand what true terror was.

The new ground-floor flat had been home for a while now, and Mike was more content than he'd ever been, apart from the strange nightmares he had where Mum appeared, coming towards him with her hand out. He reached to take it every time, and at the last second, just before his fingertips touched hers, she snatched her arm back, laughing, telling him she wouldn't hold hands with him even if it saved her life. He woke crying, unable to explain the feeling of aloneness, how empty he was, wanting love from a mother he hated. He'd spent the months at Nanny's while Dad saved, and these months at the flat so far, confused and trying to work out his contrary emotions.

The thing that bothered him the most was only having two toothbrushes in the bathroom, his and Dad's. Mum's pink one was gone, off to the man's house with her. He should have felt glad it wasn't there, mocking him from the clear plastic cup on the sink, but oddly, he missed it. Maybe, even though she was horrible to him the majority of the time, the fact that she was still there gave him some semblance of security. Made him the same as most of the other kids at school—a two-parent household. And the children who did live with just one, it was always the mum, so him being with Dad was strange, and he got the piss taken out of him. Someone had even called him a bender, and he didn't know what that meant. He'd had to ask Dad, who'd told him he wasn't one of those if he fancied girls and to ignore the lads who ribbed him.

They sat at the small table in the kitchen, eating dinner. Dad had made chicken casserole and dumplings, one of the many things Nanny had taught him while they'd stayed there. He'd got good at cooking, and it was much better than the meals Mum dished up.

"What did you do at school?" Dad popped a slice of carrot in his mouth.

Mike shrugged. "Lessons. I hate maths." And he did. He'd had to use the new compass today to create circles.

"Oh dear. But you like English, don't you?"

"Art is best. I like making dot to dots."

"Ah, that reminds me. I picked up a new book for you today. Lots of pictures for you to do."

Mike's tummy fluttered with excitement. Once a month, Dad bought him a dot-to-dot book, and each day, Mike filled only one in so it lasted until the next time he got one. "Thanks!"

"You can have it after dinner. Eat up then."

Mike tucked in, and when his belly was almost bursting, he had to give in and leave a dumpling. Dad nicked it, grinning, and they laughed. This was a good life, right here with his favourite person, yet the ideal Mike had in his head of the three of them, just as happy, wouldn't go away.

He hated her and still loved her.

A knock echoed, and Mike got up to answer it. Nanny had said she'd nip round with a strawberry trifle and maybe some sweets if he was lucky. He ran down the hallway and flung the front door open, but Nanny wasn't standing there.

"Where's your dad?" the woman said.

Mike shrank away, backing up, and he bumped into Dad behind him.

"What do you want, Peggy?" Dad pushed Mike behind him, his body a shield.

"I need to talk." She looked side to side, as if worrying someone outside would see her.

"You need to talk, do you, after what you've done to us?" Dad laughed, and it sounded horrible. "You walk out, then get a fucking loan, forging my signature and forcing us to leave our home, and you need to talk? Piss right off." He stepped forward.

Mike stood there alone, staring at her, hugging himself. Dot bounded along and sat beside him, pressing his now bigger body against his leg. Mum stared at the dog, and her eyes narrowed.

"Another fucking mutt," she mumbled.

"Whether we have another dog or not is none of your business," Dad snapped, gripping the door to close it.

She put her foot on the threshold. "Please, I have nowhere else to go."

"What do you mean? What about the new place with your fancy man?" Dad clenched the edge of the door, knuckles going white.

"He...we... I shouldn't have gone with him."

"That's the funniest thing I've heard in ages." Dad laughed again. "It didn't work out with him, so you've come crawling back? Fuck off, Peggy, you're not welcome here."

"I could cause trouble," she said.

"Could you? What, more than you already have?"

She shrugged. "Hmm."

"How the hell did you find out where we live?" Dad said.

"Easy. I followed you from work. Been standing out here for a while, waiting."

"Don't ever come here again," he said. "We don't want you."

No, we don't want you. *Mike squirmed.* But I do really, I want you to be a good mummy. *He needed a wee. His stomach hurt from all the tension.*

Dad slammed the door, and Mike let the pee out.

Dad quickly drew him into a hug. "It's all right, don't you worry, we won't see her again."

Mike cried, his legs going cold. Dad helped him out of his trousers and sent him off for a bath while he cleaned up the mess. Mike stared at the sink, at the two blue toothbrushes, and bit on his bottom lip. When he was older, he'd get some toothbrushes from ladies and keep them for the times he felt alone. He'd pretend they belonged to a mum he'd never had, one who told him he was a good boy, she loved him, and she was proud of him.

Once again, the next day, Dad found Dot in the garden, lying on his side, his tongue hanging like a thick slab of raw bacon, the tip touching the grass. She'd struck again, that evil Peggy, and Dad said he just didn't understand how the Dots could have the exact same holes in their sides when there were no thorny bushes here.

But Mike knew, and he kept quiet.

Mike snapped out of his thoughts and stared at Peggy. Her head hung limp towards her shoulder, and her tongue was like that raw pig's liver, sticking out, fat and grotesque, just like Dot number two. Shit, she was dead already—he must have zoned out like he had when he was Olivia's boyfriend. She'd hated his 'weird stare' as she'd put it. His legs were cold, and he let Peggy go, getting off her to take a look.

He'd pissed himself.

"Fucking hell," he said, stopping short of shouting it in case her neighbours heard him.

Her top was soaking, and anger gripped him. He'd been so stupid doing that, leaving evidence behind. Quickly, he stripped her, bundling the top up and stuffing it into a carrier bag she had hanging on her bedroom door handle. He'd take it home with him. Desperate to sort this out, he rushed into the bathroom and grabbed her packet of wet wipes and returned to the bedroom to wash her. Thankfully, the wee hadn't gone onto the bed covers, so he cleaned her up and put the wipes in the carrier bag, too. Next, he got her toothbrush and applied some paste, then went back in and scrubbed her tummy until it was red. He wiped the paste off. He'd have to wait for her skin to dry before he could lay the picture on top and press in all the dots.

He didn't need this hassle.

To save wasting time waiting, he took his Sharpie out and went over to her bedroom window, drawing a couple of pictures and writing some words on the sill. It reminded him of the time after Mum had come to the flat, where he'd stood there looking out onto the street after his bath to see if she was still there, staring back at him. She hadn't been, of course she hadn't, but he'd written her a letter in his notebook and added some little doodles, then threw it outside as a paper aeroplane, hoping she'd come by and pick it up.

She never did. The letter had landed in a bush and stayed stuck there between some branches until it was taken off in a gust of wind three days later. He knew, he'd seen it rise and flutter away.

Job done, he shoved the pen in his pouch and took out the compass. When he'd finished with her, he'd go out to his van and collect the things he needed to leave behind. Surely the police would know it was all about Peggy then, and they'd tell the newspapers she was an awful lady, and everyone would know.

It was what kept him going, what kept him killing all the Peggys, letting the world in on how wicked she was.

Mike was eighteen, and they still lived in the flat, him and Dad, and Mike was on his way to college down the road. Thoughts of Mum were there every day, and instead of lessening with the passage of time, they flourished, giving him hours of contemplation as to what he'd do if he ever saw her. He imagined he'd get that anxious feeling in his belly, as if he were nine all over again, or he'd cry and ask her what he'd done wrong, why she hadn't loved him. He'd asked her why she'd killed a third Dot six months after Dad had bought the cute puppy home.

At the little shop a few metres from college, he went inside to collect Dad's newspaper so he could have a read of it after work. He picked up a dot-to-dot book as well, a pastime he couldn't stop himself from doing no matter how hard he tried. And there she was, down the wine aisle, standing there holding up a bottle of red in one hand and a white in the other. She turned, slowly, and faced him, and her eyes did their usual narrowing.

Mike clutched the newspaper and book, rendered immobile by her presence. He'd come down here to get some beers to share with Dad later—Mike had a job at the supermarket four evenings a week so could afford small treats for them—but now he didn't know whether to pick up a four-pack or walk to the till, pay, and get the hell out.

"Mike?" she said, placing the bottles back on the shelf. "Is that you?"

He swivelled and walked to the cash desk, handing over the money then leaving pretty fucking quick. He stomped down the road, annoyed with the conflicting feelings swishing around inside him. He wanted to stab her; he wanted to hug her. He wanted her to want to hug him.

"Mike! Wait!"

Shit, she was bloody following him, so he veered away from the college and instead headed in the other direction, to the field opposite behind an old abandoned building, woods at the bottom. He could hide there and do a few dot pictures, get his composure back before signing in late at college, saying he'd had a doctor's appointment or whatever.

He ran across the grass and into the tree line, immediately feeling safer now he was surrounded by trunks and leaves. He kept going until he reached the centre and sat on the massive hollow log where the kids came to smoke fags on their lunchbreak. He took a pen out of his rucksack and busied himself joining the dots, and it wasn't long before the picture emerged. A blackbird with a worm dangling from its beak.

"There you are!" she said, all breathily, and came to stand in front of him in this weird skirt that had Aztec patterns all over it.

Mike scowled up at her, pissed off she'd had the guts to tail him in here. This was his private space, not hers, and now she'd tainted it.

"Get lost," he said.

"Mike, I just need to explain, and then maybe your dad will listen and I can come back."

"Explain what? I remember everything, you know. How you treated me, made me eat raw liver, how you killed my fucking dogs, you nasty piece of shit!" He flung the book and pen down and stood, towering over her, and my God, it was good to be bigger than her, stronger, the one with the upper hand.

She gasped and stepped back a pace. "I did no such thing!"

"So you've got a selective memory now, have you?" He advanced on her. "Convenient to forget, is it? Make the kid think he doesn't remember right, doesn't know what he's talking about, so you can what, wheedle your way back in?"

"No, that's not it at all. It's just children see things how they want to see them, and—"

"So you didn't kill my Dots, is that what you're saying?"

She shook her head. "Of course I didn't."

"Liar!" He punched her then, right in the face, his knuckles hurting from the impact.

She staggered, and he moved forward, arm raised to wallop her again.

"Tell me the truth, that's the least you owe me," he said. "For once, just be honest."

She pressed her back to a tree and stared at him. "All right, I killed your fucking manky dogs, and yes, I hated you, still do. Just seeing you here now, the image of your prick of a father, makes my skin crawl. I only want to come back so I have somewhere to stay until I find someone else. You're a worthless, horrible piece of shit, always have been, and I regret the day I had you. You'll never be a winner, always the loser, the one no one roots for. Bender."

"What did you say?"

"Did the kids at school call you that by any chance?"

"How do you bloody know?"

"Because," she said, smiling, "I stood at the school fence and told them to."

He grabbed her throat with one hand and squeezed, keeping her arms pinned to her front with this other. Stupid, garbled words came out of her, like please *and* don't *and* I fucking hate you *and* I wish you were dead. *But her jeans going dark from her pissing herself was enough to show him she was scared despite spouting foulness from her nasty little mouth.*

He let her throat go, still pinning her, though, and said, "All I ever wanted was for you to say sorry, but you can't manage it, can you?"

"Sorry for what?" she rasped.

"Being a bad mother."

She laughed, and it sounded as if she smoked fifty fags a day. Must have been the grip he'd had on her. And that noise, it grated, got right inside his head, and he gripped her up again, throttling the life out of the woman who'd given him his. The light went out of her eyes, and he took his hand away, staring at it in awe—it had killed Peggy all by itself, and he hadn't been able to stop it. Breathless, relieved, he dragged her to the ground and took his compass from his pencil case in his rucksack. Jabbed it in her earlobe and dragged it across until the pouch of skin came loose. He did the same with the other one, then lifted her eyelids and put the lobes beneath them.

"Can you see now? See how long those stupid earrings made your ears?"

Her once faint moustache had got darker, a fluffy brown strip, and he stabbed at it with the compass until he couldn't see it anymore. Then he stripped off her Aztec skirt, stuffing it in his rucksack so he could keep it as a memento, something of hers, even though he hated it. He heaved her to the log and stuffed her inside, pushing her feet until she was in the centre. It took a while, and he got hot and bothered but managed it in the end. He scooped up fallen leaves and packed them into the ends, loads and loads of them, hiding her from view.

He collected his dot book, the pen, the compass, and Dad's paper, and walked out of the woods, entering the college and going straight to the loos. He washed his hands, her blood going pink as it mixed with the water, and watched it swirl down the drain. In reception, he wrote in the late book that he'd overslept. He couldn't say the doctor's now in case someone found Peggy and checked his alibi. But he'd been in the shop, and they'd remember him, seeing as he nipped in there every day.

Shit. He'd have to play this by ear when he was questioned, and he couldn't imagine the police not visiting them, seeing as she'd been married to Dad.

Wiping the sweat from his brow, he went to class, nodding at the teacher as he took his seat. While the lesson progressed, instead of writing notes, he coloured in the blackbird, then, with the red pencil, he filled in the worm. He was that bird, and Peggy was that worm, all scarlet and bloodied.

Look who was the winner now.

CHAPTER SEVENTEEN

At home, Mike stood at the kitchen sink and patted Dot on the head. Her wiry fur scratched his palm, a comfort. "You're a good girl. I love you. I'm proud of you."

She whimpered and stared up at him, her complete trust in him showing in her eyes.

"Am I a good boy? And do you love me? Are you proud of me for strangling the Peggys who killed you?"

Dot wagged her tail. Yeah, she was proud of him. It helped to know someone was. He had no idea how Dad felt about him from one visit to the next. Most of the time he didn't even know who Mike was. His wife, she was a saint, despite Mike's initial feelings towards her, and she looked after Dad well, although he'd have to go in a home one day. Dementia. Dad had been robbed when Mum had left, given a respite with his new wife and children, then robbed again. He didn't deserve that—another reason to kill all the Peggys, sticking up for Dad as well as himself. That poor man also didn't deserve Mike retreating once Dad's new life had begun, but it was like being rejected all over again, same as when *she'd* done it.

A low growl rumbled from Dot, and she loped off into the hallway, sniffing at the bottom of the front door. She barked, then a knock came, and Mike wondered if this was it. Had someone seen him at the latest Peggy's? Or here, walking through the garage area with the carrier bag he'd taken from her place? He had no blood on him this time, apart from his black gloves, but no one would have seen that unless they were up close, and he hadn't been near anyone for that to happen. It was the shape behind the glass that worried him. Two shapes now he looked properly.

He moved into the living room to peer through the gap in the closed curtains. A woman with a policeman. It brought back memories, and he wasn't sure what to do. Let the coppers in like last time…or ignore them?

Sammy darted about in the woods, his heart thumping hard, laughter burbling in his windpipe. His sister, Carla, would leave her place in front of what they called The Counting Tree soon, to find him. Hide and Seek was loads of fun, but she always knew where he was. Desperate to find somewhere he'd never been before, he rushed into the small clearing, thinking to run through to the trees on the other side, where he didn't usually go.

A large log, bigger than a person, sat right in front of him. Why hadn't he thought of this before? Carla must be halfway through the count by now—fifty, fifty-one, fifty-two, I'll soon be coming to get you—so he got down on his knees ready to lie flat behind it. Twigs filled the end, and that must mean the log was hollow, so he set about yanking them free. There were so many, and he was conscious of the time ticking away, so he'd have to get a move on or abandon the log and use it on the next go round.

The twigs scratched his hands and arms, but he tugged them out and threw them aside. They were so old and gnarly. Carla would see the pile he'd made, so he quickly got up and spread them with his foot. That would have to do. Back on his knees, he put his hands on the ground and headed inside the log. A pair of old shoes were in there, high ones like his auntie pranced about in, although they didn't seem new. But that was a bit odd, wasn't it? Who'd hide shoes there? Had they walked home barefoot?

Then the sight of something frightened him, and he scuttled backwards, his heart thumping for a different reason now, and the laughter died inside him. While it didn't resemble what he knew a person to look like, it had the same shape, and the shoes made sense now.

The person hadn't gone home without them at all.

The person was still there, except they didn't seem to have any meat on them.

He screamed, his throat hurting, and Carla came bursting out of the tree line.

"What's wrong?" she said, breathless.

Sammy pointed at the log, and Carla bent over to peer inside.

"Oh my God..." She grabbed Sammy's arm, dragging him up and away. "We need to get help."

They sat on the sofa in the flat, those coppers, while Dad was in a chair. Mike stood by the window, staring out so they couldn't see his face. He knew why they were here, and in the time between killing Mum and now, two years, he'd practised his facial expressions ready for this moment. He thought he'd got it exactly right but hadn't factored in the fear.

He didn't want to go to prison, didn't want to leave Dad on his own with Dot.

"What's happened?" Dad said. "Is it my mum? Has she fallen and hurt herself?"

"It's not your mother, no. I'm afraid the remains of your ex-wife were discovered two weeks ago," the woman said.

She'd introduced herself upon arrival as DI Nabley, and the copper was Dave Wotton.

"What? Remains? Two weeks?" Dad sounded shocked, hurt maybe.

How could he be hurt when she'd *hurt him so much? Why be upset over a bitch like that? Mike was surprised she hadn't been found sooner. He'd spent every day after, waiting for it to come on the local news or be splashed in Dad's nightly paper. So much time had gone by now that he'd reckoned she'd stay hidden forever.*

Mike had gone back there on lots of occasions, and at the start, the smell alone should have given her away. The smokers no longer went there. In the common room, they'd said some animal must have died, and Mike had silently agreed with them.

Yes, Peggy was an animal.

He'd stuffed new leaf fall inside the ends of the log until winter had come and there were no more. Then he'd packed it out with branches he'd snapped from the trees, so many it was difficult to see past them unless you had a torch, and who would think to do that anyway? No one wanted to look inside logs, did they.

"I said remains because your wife had been there for some time," Nabley said. "We haven't come to *you sooner as it's taken a while to establish who she was. Tests and things, you know."*

"What's it got to do with me, though?" Dad asked. "Why are you here? I was granted a divorce after so many years of us being apart. She left us to live with another man."

"Sorry to hear that. We're here because we're speaking to everyone who knew her. While we know about your divorce through records, you were married, and therefore, you're someone who may be able to shed some light on her death. When was the last time you saw her?"

"God, I can't even remember. I know what we said to each other, but not when. That night will always stick out because I thought she was bloody rude turning up and saying what she did."

"What was your last conversation about?"

"She wanted to come back, implied she'd made a mistake. I couldn't let her. She'd not only gone off with a bloke, but she'd taken out a joint loan, forging my signature. We had the bailiffs round, and I had to stump up my half of the loan or they'd take some of our stuff away. I didn't have the money, so they removed goods, even though I told them the loan was nothing to do with me."

"Didn't you report her for fraud?"

"I wasn't interested. I just wanted her out of our lives. I told her to get lost, or words to that effect, and she left. I haven't seen her since. To be honest, I thought she'd moved away, because in a town this size, you're bound to see people from time to time, aren't you."

"She did move away, you're right," Nabley said. *"Her last known address is in Shadwell. As you probably know, she had no living relatives, and as she was adopted after years in foster care, she didn't know her real parents, so no family member even knew she was missing."*

Mike hadn't known Peggy was adopted. Did that make a difference to how he felt?

No, she still shouldn't have treated him like that. And why had she behaved that way towards him when she'd had instability in her life? It didn't make sense. If she'd been pushed from pillar to post in the foster system, wouldn't she want to prevent her child from feeling unloved and unwanted?

He licked his teeth.

"A work colleague reported her missing two years ago," Nabley went on. *"No trace of her was found until recently."*

"What do you mean by remains?" Dad's voice shook.

Mike imagined his hands did, too.

"It wasn't a body as such. It's estimated she actually died at the time she was reported missing. Thereabouts anyway. It's difficult to get a certain time of death once years have passed. More specifically, and this may upset you, she was murdered. Her hyoid bone was broken."

"What's that?"

"A bone in the neck."

"Oh Jesus. Christ...she was strangled?"

"She was. I have to ask this, standard procedure, but where were you two years ago?" She gave the dates of the week Mike had killed her.

His stomach muscles contracted. They'd managed to get it so close to that day.

"I've got no idea," Dad said. "Who the hell would? I could ring up my work and ask them."

"Please do that."

Mike held his breath while Dad chatted to his boss.

"Do you want to speak to him?" Dad asked. "He says I went to Lincoln on a plumbing job for that whole week."

Nabley spoke for a while, the one-sided conversation not giving much away, and Mike turned slightly to watch her. She nodded a lot, hmmed, then handed the phone back to Dad, who ended the call and put the phone on the cradle.

"What about in the evenings of that week, Mr Redmond?" Nabley asked. "Now you've had your memory jogged about the daytime, where would you have been at night?"

"I haven't had my memory jogged at all. A job in Lincoln means nothing if the work wasn't anything that stands out. If we're talking a boiler explosion, then yes, I'd remember, but not the smaller things. So I'd have been at home. I don't go out, see. The only night I can verify that is the Wednesday, because Mike here didn't work at the supermarket on those nights. He's with me now, my apprentice, so no more shelf stacking for him."

Dad was talking too much, and Mike worried it would make them think he'd done it, that he'd strangled that whore and stuffed her in the log.

"What about you, Mike?" she said, standing and coming over to him.

He forced some tears out and faced her. "I'd have been at college then. Like Dad, I can't remember that far back. Two years is a long time."

"Okay, that's easy enough to check. I suppose the college will have computerised registers or something to show attendance."

Mike thought back to about six months after he'd killed her. The college computer system had gone down, wiping everything. Something about a server malfunction.

He was safe. Fucking safe!

"Are you all right?" Nabley rested a hand on his shoulder.

Mike nodded. "It's just, even though she left us, she was still my mum." That sounded plausible, and he wasn't lying. She was *still his mum, regardless of the shit she'd put him through. She didn't deserve his warped loyalty, but there you go.*

"I understand, and I'm so sorry to have brought you this news."

Nabley and Wotton left after having a cup of tea—why didn't they fuck off sooner?—with promises to keep them updated if they wanted that. Dad didn't, and neither did Mike. He told them he'd laid her to rest a long time ago—hahaha—and didn't need to do it again.

But he did *need to do it again. That urge to kill her over and over was still there inside him, and he didn't think it would ever go away. Not until he acted it out.*

So he bought an A4 pad and let the plotting begin.

In case those people wanted to come in like last time, Mike kicked the carrier bag with the pissy wet wipes and Peggy's clothes in it under the sofa, took the peg dolls off the mantel, and the dot-to-dot frames off the wall, and hid them under a cushion on his chair. He needed to catch up and make the other dolls, but he'd been so busy, then tired after killing, that he hadn't had the energy. The Aztec-patterned skirt with parts cut off was draped over the back of the sofa, and he stuffed it in the cupboard of the TV unit.

He had no time to go in the kitchen and put the board away where he'd drawn the suitcase, nor could he get rid of the beard, moustache, and his hairy cap. He shut the kitchen door, so no one was tempted to be nosy, and stopped at the sight of the black bin liner in the hallway with the boiler suit inside.

"Fuck," he whispered.

He chucked it in the cupboard under the stairs then opened the front door, purposely raising his eyebrows at the sight of the woman in normal clothes and the man in a uniform. It could be Nabley and Wotton all over again, except their hair was a different colour.

"Blimey, what's going on?" He glanced out into the street as though searching for the source of the issue: a neighbour having a fight, or a car being stolen.

"Hello. I'm DC Lara Kenilworth, and this is PC Quinn. Nothing to worry about, we're just talking to people who own white vans. You have one registered to you, yes?"

"Yep, it's for work," he said.

"Would you mind if we had a look at it?" she asked, head cocked.

He'd brought his special bag inside, so he was safe, and his pouch was under his mattress. "No problem. I'll just get the keys." He reached across and took them out of the little box on the wall. The house keys were on the bunch. "Just need to get my shoes on, won't be a sec." He left the door open so they could see him doing it, nothing to hide here, motherfuckers. "It's out the back, though, in Bluebird Avenue."

"Why's it there?" she asked.

He stepped outside and closed the door. "My garage has my car in it, and the people round here get funny if you park in front of it. Clogs up the area apparently. Come on, I'll show you." He led the way down the alley, then by the garages. "That's my one there." He pointed to the red door. "My van's through here." Out in Bluebird, he stood by the van, hoping the fact he was shitting himself didn't show on his face. The net must be drawing in if they'd got wind of him owning a white van. Someone along the way must have seen him parked outside a Peggy house. Or was it that bloody postman?

He handed the keys to Kenilworth. She took them and went straight to the back, opening the doors. She peered inside, while Quinn squinted through the driver's-side window.

"Can I open your toolbags?" she asked.

"Yep. Mind yourself, though. There's a sharp file in there."

She took gloves from her pocket—*why?*—and moved various things around. "Ah, that's fine. I appreciate you letting me do this."

"Can I ask what this is about? Bit weird for the police to be nosing in vans, isn't it?"

"It's an ongoing enquiry," she said. "There's nothing for you to worry about."

But there is. "Fair enough."

She locked up, gave the keys back, and Quinn shook his head as if to tell her there wasn't anything in the front either. There wouldn't be.

"We'll leave you to it then," Kenilworth said.

Mike bobbed his head and walked towards the garages.

"Oh, just one thing…"

He turned. Kenilworth and Quinn came abreast of him, one either side. That was a tad intrusive, his personal space violated, but what could he do?

"What's that then?" He continued on, sliding his hands in his pockets in case they had a mind to shake. He idly wondered if that move bothered them, whether they thought he'd pull a knife out.

"What have you been doing today?" She gave the sort of smile that said: *Sorry, got to ask.*

"Off sick." He shrugged and ran his tongue over his teeth. This was getting to him. "Reckon I've got the flu coming. Woke up rough, thought it best I stay home. Today's job was at a school, and I don't want to be passing whatever it is to the kids." He was great at lying. All those years of practise, keeping Mum's 'gone' secret.

"Makes sense."

He headed down the alley and waited for them at his gate. "Is that it then? Only, I could do with getting back on the sofa. Need a kip."

"Yes, and thank you for your time."

"No problem."

He walked up his path and didn't look back. It'd seem well dodgy if he did. Inside, he went to the living room window and peered out through the curtain gap. They'd gone up the road a bit, to the other side, and knocked on the door of some bloke who also owned a white van. Mike relaxed. They really were checking them all, not just his.

Relieved, he took the peg dolls out and stood them on the mantel. Hung the pictures back up. Instead of the nap he'd mentioned, he sat and made the other dolls, shuddering at the feel of the Aztec material when he cut some out for the dresses. He'd have five in a row soon, but while he was at it, he'd make one for Mum. After all, she was the first Peggy, and she needed to be with the others. All bitches together.

CHAPTER EIGHTEEN

Tracy stood in front of the whiteboards after adding the most recent information. "Where are we with the people who live by Deirdre Kaggle?"

Erica checked her notebook. "No one noticed anything out of the ordinary—they all work full time, so any white vans in the area, they wouldn't have seen unless it was at night."

Tim tapped his pen on the desk. "But like they said, they get home, shut the curtains and the world out, and that's that."

"Bugger." Tracy rubbed her forehead. "And now my phone's going off. Great." She took it out of her pocket. Lara's name was on the screen. "Hi, have you got something?"

"No. Me and Quinn have spoken to twenty-three men so far about the vans, and none of them seem iffy. All have allowed us to look inside them. The other officers have the same feedback, I'm afraid. I'm just ringing to let you know the score. We'll carry on with the others on the list, but they're going to roll over to tomorrow. There are too many people."

"Okay, thanks, and don't forget to take a breather. Eat. You still get meal breaks even when some bastard's haring around murdering people."

"Yep, we'll go now. One of them owns a burger van, so that's handy."

"Stay out until four, then come back and do your paperwork."

"Will do. Bye!"

Tracy slid her phone away and told the rest of the team what Lara had said. "So we're still stuck in place. What about the CCTV, Alastair?"

"Nothing on any of the routes around the victims' homes. I'm now going farther afield to check vehicles outside the areas. There has to be a camera somewhere."

"We've got uniforms in the streets in question, looking for home CCTV," she said. "You'd think, with all the shit that goes on these days, more people would have their own security. So far, sod all. The cameras on view are all dummies."

"So he's obviously worked out his route, ensuring there's no CCTV," Alastair said.

"Yep." Tracy nodded. "What about social media, girls?" She glanced from Nada to Erica.

"There's nothing weird on any of their platforms," Nada said. "Digi forensics are going through their accounts, laptops, and phones in more detail, but if they haven't got back to us yet, I'd say they've come up blank."

"We could do with finding private messages revealing worries about them being watched," Damon said. "At least then we'd know for sure whether it's random kills or they're on some kind of list."

"Could be either." Tracy went over to the coffee machine to make them all a drink. "All the victims have the same colour hair, or as near as anyway. That means something. If we think about what we suspect so far, that hair belongs to a female who featured in the killer's life at some point. There's the little boy and the dad in the house picture, the lad under a bed with a dog. There aren't any images of the woman, which tells me our man is fixated on him perhaps being with his father all the time, or he is the father and he's alone with his son. The wife/mother isn't in the picture, pardon that pun there, and the father/husband can't get over that. Tell me if I'm away with the fucking fairies here, will you?"

"Anything's plausible," Damon said.

"Yep, nutters have all sorts of reasons, don't they." Alastair shook his head. "The women having the same hair is a classic with most serial killers. I did my profile refresher course the other week, as you know, and there are so many crimes related to hair or eyes, even height, and one, they were fixated on hands. They had to have big knuckles. I mean what's that all about?"

"That one bothered me, too," Erica said. "And the one with bunions."

Tracy clapped. "Nice as a change of subject is, it's not really helping. No big knuckles and bunions on our women. We should—" She took a deep breath. "For fuck's sake. Give me a second." She answered her annoying as eff phone again. "Hello there, Vic. What crap are you going to throw at us now? Joke, by the way." It wasn't, she'd just said it to save herself from looking a cow, although her team were well used to her by now. Still, after Paul had sniped at her, she reckoned she'd make a conscious effort to tone the snark down. When she remembered to. If she felt like it.

"Missing woman report has just come in," Vic said.

She shuddered from a cold shiver going up her back. "Go on."

"A Rona Dandridge. Now, she's only just missing, hence us not pressing the panic button at the moment, but I thought I'd tip you off. She didn't turn up for work, and she's never off ill or anything, but it was her hair that got to me. Her boss emailed an image of Rona that they have on file, and she's a bit like the ladies in your case. I'm probably jumping the gun, but…"

"No, no, you did the right thing. I can look into it, and if it's nothing to do with us, no harm done, and missing persons can continue dealing with it, although I will say, she could have just overslept."

"She starts work at twelve, though."

"I see. Did the boss say anything else?"

"That Rona goes to the gym every morning. Muscle Mania."

"Fucking hell, who thinks up these stupid names? Okay, leave it with me. What's her address, please?"

"Nineteen Pelican Place."

The fucking bird estate again. A link or just me hoping for one? "Rightio. And her work address and boss' name?"

"Nigel Stepton, File Things."

"What's that then?"

"Files and things to do with them." Vic laughed.

"Serves me right for asking a divvy question. Catch you soon." She swiped her screen. "I've got to make a couple of calls. Possible new victim, but let's not put and two and two together just yet." She went into her office so she could concentrate better—*and* so the expectant stares from her team didn't get her back up. She didn't need the pressure.

She sat at her desk and wiggled her mouse. The monitor came to life, and she did a search for the address and phone number for Muscle Mania and wrote it down. She did the same for File Things and rang Mr Stepton first.

"Hello, sir. DI Tracy Collier. You spoke to my colleague about a missing person after you contacted that department, yes?"

"I did. Like I said to him, Rona is *never* off, even when she's ill. I've phoned her mobile and landline, and she's not picking up. I also called her mother after I spoke to the man at the police station. Vic, I think it was."

"Yes, that's right. What did her mother have to say?"

"She agreed with me that this isn't like Rona, so she's going to go round there and see if she's too poorly to phone in sick."

"Right, that's great. Contact me if you hear from her." She gave him her number.

"Will do. Bye now."

Next she dialled Muscle Mania. If Rona had been to the gym as usual, something was possibly off, although she could have a secret wicked streak in her and had decided to skive work for the first time.

"Muscle Mania, Toni Morin, how may I help you?"

Too fucking jolly for words, love. "Hello, my name is Detective Inspector Tracy Collier, and I'm calling to ask if a Rona Dandridge has been to the gym today. Would you even be aware of that?"

"Oh yes, Rona was in. She did her session, then we had a little set-to in reception."

"A set-to? What about?"

"Her direct debit had been declined for her monthly subscription, and I had to ask if she was going to pay it in cash, plus for the days she'd used our services since the money didn't go through. She got upset, as you can imagine."

"What time was that?"

"Let me just check. I wrote it down. Ah, here we are. Eleven-fifteen."

"Do you know if she drives to the gym?"

"No, sorry."

"Okay, thank you for your help." Tracy went back to the incident room. "Right, do me a favour, Nada. Get on Facebook and see if a Rona Danridge has a page. I want to know when she last posted. Alastair, look into any possible vehicles she owns. Erica, you're on any priors. Tim, get on the other social media sites. Damon, we may well be going to Rona's house in a bit, so go and have a wee or whatever."

She left the room and did the same, then nipped to Chief Winter's office. She was way behind schedule in bringing him up to date and braced herself for a bollocking. Oddly, he was okay about the time lapse.

"You always have things in hand," he said. "Good luck in finding whoever it is. I'll think about the wording for a press release and deal with that so you can get on. It's in *The Herald*, you say?"

"Unfortunately, yes, and there's quite a bit of info, so a police source didn't go off the record with what information they were prepared to release. Andy Babbitt thinks I'm incompetent, that women DIs are useless, and feels him and the community can solve it themselves."

"Babbitt can piss off." Winter smiled.

"Thanks for being understanding, sir."

She left and returned to the incident room, her phone jangling in her pocket. "Yep?"

"Sorry, me again," Vic said.

"What have you got?"

"Dispatch just called. Rona's mother rang them. She went round to her daughter's house. The door was ajar and—"

"Shit!"

"Everything all right?"

"No, it bloody well isn't. The door being open is a feature of these murders. You're going to tell me she's dead, aren't you?"

"Afraid so."

"Arseholes. We'll go there now." She stowed her phone away. "Rona's been found—deceased. Quickly, what did you find out?"

"She drives a Kia," Alastair said.

"Her other social media apart from Facebook is Instagram." Tim. "She hasn't posted on Insta for two days."

"No priors," Erica said.

"She posted on Facebook this morning—she has a public page." Nada leant towards her monitor. "She wrote: *God, I'm so bloody angry. @Muscle Mania are expecting me to pay double because my bloody direct debit bounced. So that's thirty quid to pay for the bounced amount, plus thirty for the days I've used since. Bloody daylight robbery. Grr. I'm going to the sports centre instead.*

At least then I can go swimming and stuff as well. Then she has an angry face emoji, plus a knife."

"Any comments?" Tracy asked.

Nada recited them. "She didn't respond after Phil with the Skill's suggestive comment."

"Right, me and Damon will go there now. Alastair, I want CCTV checked. There has *got* to be a camera by that gym. I want to know when she arrived, when she left, and where she went afterwards. Someone somewhere intercepted her along the way—and let's face it, that's got to be what happened if she was at the gym arguing with the receptionist at eleven-fifteen. She starts work at twelve, so that's limited time for her to go home and get ready. Everyone else, you know the drill. Come on, Damon."

Tracy had the sense of wanting to rush, although what was the point when Rona was dead? Still, once they were in the car, she gunned the engine and sped off to Pelican Place, her lights flashing so people got the hell out of the way.

"Blimey, what's with the speed?" Damon said.

"I don't know." She eased her foot off the accelerator. "Maybe I'm hoping the killer is hanging around, who knows."

"I doubt it very much, but I get where you're coming from. It's this desperate feeling that this needs to come to an end. If Rona is one of our girls, that's five of them since Sunday, and that's one hell of a man on a mission. What's he planning, to kill all the women who have that hair colour?"

"I bloody hope not! L'Oréal will have an uptick in blonde and black dye sales soon if he does, maybe even pink and purple if the women are feeling particularly daring. We'll have a load of rainbow heads on the streets."

They laughed, Tracy a bit maniacally. The hard work and tossing and turning she'd done last night were taking a toll.

She pulled up behind a patrol car outside number nineteen and got out, approaching York who stood on the pavement in front of a woman who sat on the wall—Rona's wall, where there might be evidence.

You stupid little cow! "We'll need to move away from here, ladies." She stared at York. "This wall is part of a crime scene."

York flushed, as she well might, and helped the lady shuffle along to the next house. Tracy checked the entrance to the garden. At least the useless baggage had tied tape to the gate this time. Damon, in a protective suit and gloves, opened it and put booties on, then entered the house.

"Mrs Danridge?" Tracy asked.

She nodded. "P-Pam."

"Okay, Pam, I'm going to ask you some questions in a moment, but I need to speak to my colleague here first, all right?" Tracy walked off and waited for York to join her beneath a tree several metres away. "I'm not even going to go off at you about the wall, you know you messed up. What's the score here?"

York's cheeks went even redder. "I'm sorry. Really sorry."

Okay, I wasn't going to go off, but...I lied. "You always are, but you can't be that sorry if you're not changing your behaviour." She should be telling herself that, too. "Now shut up about that and tell me what's what."

"The call came in that Pam Danridge had found her daughter. I came out, went inside, and Pam was sitting on Rona's bedroom floor, crying. The bed had been moved because Rona was under it. I checked for a pulse, nothing. Then I brought Pam out here and asked her what had happened."

"Right. Notice anyone about in the street? Any white vans?"

"No, and to be honest, I was too busy getting inside."

"Fine. Where's Robbie—I take it he's with you?"

"He's round the back checking if someone broke in that way."

Tracy strode off to Pam, wincing at the SOCO van turning up. It might distress the woman further. "Pam, can you tell me what happened?"

She sniffled. "After Rona's boss rang me, I got worried. I tried ringing Rona, but she didn't answer, so I came straight here. I was worried"—she hiccoughed a sob—"worried she was ill and couldn't get hold of her phone. The door was open a bit, and that frightened me to death. I read the paper about those women and the doors being like that, and I knew she was dead, just knew it, but I tried to tell myself she wasn't." She moaned, the sound so full of grief. "So I went in, and she wasn't downstairs. I thought she might be bundled up on the sofa, you know, watching films with some Lucozade like I used to give her as a little girl. I hoped...hoped she was, but she wasn't, and I checked her bedroom and...and she was there and she...she..."

"Okay, Pam. Take a deep breath. Don't think about Rona like that now. Think about when you got here. Did you see anyone in the street?"

"No." She shook her head as if that proved she hadn't. "No."

"Do you have someone who can take you home? I don't think you should be driving in this state."

"My son."

"And is there someone else who can drive your car if you'll be in his?"

"His wife."

"Do you want me to phone them?"

"No, it needs to come from me. I should be the one to do it."

Tracy glanced at Paul, who was suiting up at Rona's front door. He didn't look pleased at being called to yet another scene when he'd barely got to work at the previous. Robbie came along, and she sent him on house-to-house.

"I need to go inside now, okay?" she said to Pam. "You stay with Simone York here, and she'll come round later for a proper statement." She stared at York: *And don't fuck it up.* What she actually said to her was, "Get someone here to do the log at the door. Keep your eye out until they arrive, then help Robbie." And to Pam, "I'm sorry for your loss, and we're doing everything we can to find this man."

"Thank you."

York nodded, and Tracy went to the SOCO van and got clothing out, putting it on quickly. She closed the gate behind her and waited for a SOCO to go inside the house, then followed him. Paul stood at the top of the stairs, looking down.

"It's the same," he said.

With a heavy heart, Tracy went up there. When was this going to end?

CHAPTER NINETEEN

Mike couldn't settle, even after making the latest dolls and singing *We All Stand Together* by Paul McCartney and The Frog Chorus. The six of them stared back at him from their mantel perch. He'd licked his teeth until they felt *so* smooth, yet still he found it hard to relax. He'd got the jitters from the coppers being here, no question, but what was he supposed to do about that? Should he stop killing the Peggys and wait until all this had died down? Or continue anyway, seeing as they'd spoken to the bloke over the road about *his* van, too?

If someone had seen him outside a house, they'd be looking for a bloke with long hair, a moustache, and in the last case, a beard. That was nothing like his real, bald, clean-shaven self.

That was it then. He'd carry on.

There was still plenty of time in the day to go and call on the next woman, but he needed to wait until she got back from work. She lived in a high-rise, bottom floor, easy access from the back. It was by a stretch of the canal, and he could park in the trees beside it, behind her place, and run across and into her garden. She never locked the gate in the fence, the stupid cow, so he'd get in easy.

There was something he needed to do first, though. He hadn't seen Dad in ages, and because of those bloody coppers, he had the strange sensation that if he didn't visit Dad today, he'd never see him again. That would be true if Mike got put in prison. There was no way his stepmother would take Dad to a place like that.

Mike took his clean enforcement agent uniform out of the wardrobe and placed it on the bed ready, so it was there and waiting as soon as he got back. There was a stubborn splash of blood on the stab vest, in the white trim at the top of a breast pocket, and he just couldn't get it off no matter how much he sponged it. Mind you, it was brown now, and faded, so it'd be all right. People might think it was HP Sauce.

He ushered Dot out for a wee and had one himself, then let her back in again. The hound made a move to jump up and put her paws on his shoulders, and he held a hand out to stop her.

"Do you want to come and see Dad, too?"

That would be nice, wouldn't it, a real family get-together.

Dot wagged her tail, and he thought of all the others, the exact breed as her, and how they could be the same dog if he pretended three of them hadn't been killed. Peggy had stabbed them with the compass, but she must have strangled them with the way their necks were bent all funny, and he'd choked her the same way so she knew how it felt to be a Dot.

"Come on then," he said.

She sat while he put on her collar and lead, then they were off, out to his car. He drove to Dad's, thinking about the far past as well as the more recent, and one memory overrode all the others. How he hated that.

"Get the cheese out," Mum said, "and don't take your time about it."

The early morning sun streamed in through the kitchen window, and Mike squinted. He'd only just got up and come down into the kitchen, and there she was, telling him what to do. Dad would have already left for work by now, so they were alone, and that was a dangerous time.

"Get a fucking move on, you bloody moron," she snapped, waving the cheese knife about.

He didn't like that knife. It had two points on the end, and he didn't understand why, and the blade curved. He reckoned it looked like a flat elephant's trunk, same as the one in his latest dot-to-dot book.

Mike hurried to the fridge, and in his attempt to get the cheese out fast, he dropped it on the floor. He crouched to pick it up, then Mum was down there with him, squishing his face with her hard fingers and thumb, her nails digging into his cheeks.

"I swear, you're such a useless little fucker." She brandished the knife, poking it towards him, the points so close to his nose they almost touched it. Her coffee breath was strong and warm. "One slip of my hand, and these prongs here will go either side of your septum. Know what one of those is?"

He stared at her fuzzy moustache and tried to shake his head, but her grip was too firm. She had sleepy dust in the corner of one eye, and he wanted to punch her there so it would fall off.

"Thicko. It's the middle bit between your nostrils. Want me to cut it, do you?"

"No," he managed, his lips in a pout from her mean squeeze.

"One day, I'll creep into your room while you're asleep and do it. And guess what? You'll bleed, choke on all that blood, and die!" She smirked. "So kip with one eye open if you want to live, you got that?"

"Yes."

"When I was little, there was this man, and he used to scare me with a knife. He told me a similar thing, except he said he'd use just the very end of the tip and poke holes in me so I ended up a colander, and all the blood would come out in a hundred arcs. Same as when the animals are 'gone'. I can do that to you, if you like."

"No," he whimpered.

"Then don't keep pissing me off." She moved the blade from side to side. "Remember this knife and what I said. If you do, you'll be safe. If you don't? Blood."

She pushed him backwards, and he fell on the floor. His head banged on the block of cheese. Dot dashed in and nipped Mum's arm.

"You fucking filthy creature!" She shoved the pup away.

Crying, rising to his knees and trying not to get snot anywhere, Mike picked the cheese up and handed it to her. She snatched it and pushed off the floor, walking to where she'd been making his sandwiches for his lunchbox.

"I fucking hate you," she whispered.

Mike didn't think he was meant to hear her, something deep inside told him that, so he went to the table and sat in his place to eat the cold toast. All the butter had melted, and there was something else on there, but he just couldn't work it out. Red, like jam.

"Eat it all up now," she said, slicing the cheese. "Waste not, want not."

He bit into the toast, and the familiar taste of raw liver spread out on his tongue.

"I blended that just for you." She glanced over her shoulder. "If I had to eat it as a child, then so do you."

Mike continued to chew through the tears—tears that stung his eyes and were hot on his cheeks. He didn't know what he'd done to deserve such a horrible mummy, but at least he had Dad and Dot. And Nanny. They were all a little boy needed.

Weren't they?

Mike pressed the bell at Dad's and held Dot's lead tight. She had a habit of launching herself at his stepmother, Willy, although her full name was Wilhelmina, but she said that was a bit of a mouthful and no fun at all.

Mike suddenly wished he'd been kinder to her over the years, less surly. She was nice to him regardless of how he treated her, and that said something, didn't it? She wasn't even his real mother, yet she was kinder to him than Peggy had ever been. It said a lot about her character, about how much she must love Dad if she was willing to put up with Mike being such a wanker.

She opened the door, and her smile said it all. She was pleased to see him, as usual, and her crouching to grab Dot around the neck and hug her was all the proof Mike needed that she was a good person.

She stood and hugged Mike, too. "How lovely to see you." She stepped back. "Come in, come in, your dad's going to be so happy you're here."

That was a lie, and they both knew it.

It was time to play the game of pretend.

There was no admonishment that he didn't visit much, just pleasure that he had arrived today, a happy moment in the here and now. He acknowledged to himself that he'd been off with her because he couldn't trust a mother figure, could never allow himself to love her like he'd stupidly loved Peggy, despite the way she'd hated him.

"He's in the living room," Willy said. "Let me take Dot to the kitchen for some treats while you have a chat. Cheese all right?"

Mike's heart thudded. "No. No cheese." That had come out harsher than he'd intended.

"All right then, what about—?"

"It's okay. Cheese is okay." He shouldn't have snapped at her about it. After all, she didn't know of the association, or how he'd thought of the cheese-and-knife incident on the way here. She didn't know many things, and he could hardly blame her for that. He'd never opened up to her.

Maybe he should.

No, it was too late now. Things had gone too far.

He walked in and closed the door.

She took hold of Dot's lead. "Are you sure about the cheese? I don't want to give it to her if it'll upset her tummy."

"I'm sure."

She beamed. "This way, lovely Dotty. Guess what Willy has for you. Yes, you know, don't you." She took the dog down the hallway, Dot wagging her tail like mad.

He should have known Willy was all right, a good sort. Dot wouldn't like her if she wasn't. The first Dot hadn't gone near Mum. They said dogs sensed evil, didn't they.

Mike took a deep breath then let it out slowly. He moved to stand in the living room doorway. Dad sat in his recliner, as usual, by the window so he could see outside. Mike's eyes stung, and he blinked and swallowed. He shouldn't have come, it always upset him, but he'd needed to do it, so here he was.

He went in, and Dad turned his head, no sign of recognition. No frown, just a blank face.

"Hi, Dad, it's me, Mike."

"Hello, Mike, nice to meet you. Friend of Peggy's, are you?"

Oh God, he was back *there*, thinking he was still married to her. That happened sometimes and was one of the main reasons Mike didn't want to spend even a minute with him. It was too painful.

"Not bloody likely. I don't like Peggy." Mike sat on the sofa and fiddled with the zip of his jacket. It was like Dad wasn't Dad and Mike didn't know him. They were strangers, and the dad he knew was in the past.

"Me neither." Dad glanced at the door as though Peggy would come in any second and catch him talking about her. "She's a bitch."

Mike stopped a laugh from barking out. "She is."

"She's cruel to animals, that one." Dad copied Mike and played with the zip of his cardigan. "She used to stab my son's puppies."

Mike's whole body went cold. What? Dad *knew*? All this time Mike had been hiding it from him so Peggy didn't come and kill him, and he'd been aware of it? He cleared his throat. "That's not very nice, is it."

"No, and she strangled them, too."

So Mike had suspected right. He wanted to shoot up, get Dot, and leave, but equally, he wanted to know what else Dad had to say. "That's terrible, that is."

"She told me," Dad said, "in little notes she posted through the letterbox. I still have them. Want to see?"

Mike nodded. He didn't want to see, and he did want to see, and it confused him. "All right."

Dad got up and shuffled over to the mahogany wall cabinet. He opened a drawer and ferreted inside it. "I recognised her writing. She always thinks I'm stupid." He pulled out a roll of paper tied with a pink ribbon. "Here we are. Take a look at those and tell me it's not her."

Mike took them, his hand shaking, and tugged the ribbon slowly while Dad went back to his chair. They'd been written on spiral notepad sheets, the tops ragged where they'd been ripped away, and because they'd been in a roll for so long, Mike couldn't stop them from curling back up. He flattened them in a pile on his thigh, holding them down one side.

You shouldn't have a dog. Now look what's happened. It's dead. I stabbed the little fucker then strangled it. Don't get another one. If you do, you're next.

So she'd threatened Dad as well as Mike? He felt sick—with childhood fear that seeing her writing had produced and anger that she'd tricked them both. But he shouldn't have been surprised. This was the way she'd worked.

So you got another one. WHAT DID I TELL YOU? Don't you care that I'll be coming for you now? That kid of yours doesn't deserve a pet, he doesn't deserve anything, so the animals have to go, got it? I swear, one more dog, and you're toast.

An image of him eating the raw, mushed liver on toast went through his mind, and he almost scrunched the notes up but had one more left. He pushed himself to see what it said, even though it'd upset him.

Look, this is your FINAL WARNING. Are you listening? Why do you keep getting him a dog? They smell and leave hairs everywhere, and they lick you when they've been cleaning their bums. That's not good, so stop buying the fucking things! God, I'm going to enjoy stabbing you with a compass if you DISOBEY ME.

She sounded demented, especially using capitals, and he knew, now he was an adult, that she had been. She'd passed the badness on to him, and instead of throwing it out, never to be seen again, he carried it gladly, a vile heirloom that burned within and gave him the energy he needed to keep killing her.

"These are awful," he said.

Dad nodded, attention outside. "They are. I should have told someone she wasn't right in the head, but who would believe me?"

"Nanny would."

"And she did. I wish I'd listened to her from the start."

Mike smiled at an image of her in his head. Her squidgy cuddles. How she loved him. "She made nice strawberry trifle."

"The best."

"And she taught you how to cook when we lived with her."

"When did you live with her then?" Dad frowned and stroked his smooth chin. Willy must have shaved him today. "I don't remember her having a lodger."

Mike shrugged. "Maybe you forgot."

Dad drummed his fingers on the chair arm. "Maybe I did."

"So how have you been?" Mike rolled the notes up, tight, as if that would stop the words coming loose and falling out.

"So-so. Can't complain." He rubbed his nose. "If you don't like Peggy, why are you here? She'll be home soon, you know. She'll have pizza, no doubt, but me and my boy won't be getting any."

"Came to see you, didn't I." Mike tied the ribbon, wondering if it was Peggy's. He didn't recall her putting any in her hair.

Dad craned his neck closer to the window. "That's nice of you, but I have no idea who you are."

"I know you don't." Mike threw the roll in the drawer.

"There's a man out there, mowing the grass in just his underpants. He'll freeze his nuts off. Some people, eh?"

Mike opened his mouth to reply, but Dot came galloping in and flew at Dad, landing on his lap, her size engulfing him.

"Ah, you soppy date," Dad said. "How's my Dot, eh? How are you, pretty girl? How's that paw now? All healed from the glass, is it?"

Why did he remember her and Peggy but not Mike?

That stung more than he thought possible.

"You should go out there and bite that silly man's arse, Dot. Would you like that?" He chuckled. "Young man? How come you have Dot?" Dad asked.

"I'm minding her for a bit." Mike played along. Didn't want to confuse the old boy. The look on his face when he didn't understand something hurt Mike's heart. Well, the soft bit he had left at any rate.

Dad scratched the dog's belly, and her leg went mental, pawing the air. "She's a good one, this pup. They all were until she— Let's not talk about that." He pushed Dot down to the floor so she could settle between his legs. He stroked her head, and Dot put her paw on his knee. "Where's the fella who owns her then?"

"Mike? He's busy."

"I felt sorry for him when he was a lad. Had a nice dad but a wicked mother. Peggy, her name was."

"I know."

"Bitch."

"Yep."

Willy came in, and Dot scrambled away from Dad to barrel into her.

"Having a nice catch-up, are you?" She reached down to fuss the dog.

"You can't just waltz in here! Who are you?" Dad's forehead crinkled.

"Just some woman who married you, that's all. Don't you worry about it."

"What's your name?"

"Willy."

Dad roared with laughter, his cheeks going pink. "But that's a man's dick!" He held his stomach and chortled. "Blimey, comes to something when you can marry a willy. Times have changed, I'll say that much."

"It's really Wilhelmina, you silly bugger," she said.

"I used to know a Wilhelmina once. Pretty thing. She married a man and had two kids with him. Nice of her, seeing as he was divorced and already had a son."

"Yes, that was nice of her," Willy said. "Some women are."

Mike couldn't hack this. It was fucking dreadful. "I've got to go. I'm sorry." He shot up, taking Dot's lead handle from where Willy must have tied it to her collar. He couldn't even go over and kiss his dad on the head. It was too much. So many feelings. He rushed out to the front door, fumbling to get the bloody thing open.

"Let me help you," Willy said behind him.

He moved away so she could do the honours, then stepped outside, tears streaming.

"It's okay to be upset, you know," Willy said. "I cry at least once every day, sometimes more. You love the man he was, so to see the man he is now…it's hard."

He stared at the street, at what Dad was probably looking at right now, the man mowing his grass in just his shorts, despite the weather. "I'm sorry. For everything. You dealing with him, and with me being such a tosser, the past, and what's to come in the future. At least now, when Dad finds out I've been bad, he won't remember who I am, so it won't hurt him."

"Bad? You're not bad, love."

Oh, I am. "I've never been much cop, my mum told me that, and I've proved it by being a bastard lately, but I just can't stop myself. It's her fault."

"It's all right, I understand. Maybe you could come round and see your sisters another time, eh? Shame they're not home at the minute."

"Maybe." But he wouldn't. "And for what it's worth, unlike Dad, I don't think you're a dick."

Willy threw her head back and laughed. "Oh, you are funny, just like him."

But he wasn't funny, not at all. He was messed up, sad, and didn't know how to deal with things. "See you."

He walked away, Dot at his heels, crying at Willy's "Love you!" that chased him down the path and wrapped him in a smidgen of happiness. At last, a mum who cared, but it was too late. He'd crossed a line, and there was no going back now.

CHAPTER TWENTY

Tracy couldn't stomach looking at Rona on the floor any longer. Her bed was propped against a wall. She'd been strangled, which was a given with this killer, and she had the dots on her, the earlobes and eyebrows put in the usual places, but other than that, nothing else had been done to her. No brutal whipping here, no broken nose, no sliced arm or a room full of blood. Tracy didn't need to send a picture to Nada for her to join the dots up. It was obvious what it was: a bird. The beak was drawn, as was a worm hanging out of it, and spindly legs with claws stuck out from the dotty curve of the lower belly. A fluffy toy dog sat by her head, the nose pressed to her ripped ear, as though snuffling it.

The clues meant nothing but a headache for Tracy.

She joined Paul at the window. He'd said five minutes ago there was something she needed to see, but as was her way if people insisted she do something because they wanted her to, she'd made him wait. She'd cut off her nose to spite her face doing that before, but it was ingrained in her and a habit she didn't think she'd break. That was another thing to put on her list: Stop being pedantic.

On the centre section of the uPVC sill was black writing and a couple of drawings. One what she thought was a triangle of cheese, the type with holes in it, possibly added so it was clear what the image was. A knife sat beside it, like Nada had described, two points and a curve. The other pic was three dogs, their fur longish and sticking up in all directions. As for the wording, she took a deep breath and read it.

Mummy, this is Mike, or maybe you might want to call me Scamp like Gabby does.

When will you be coming back? I know you don't like me, and even though you pick on me, I still like you a tinsy bit, because if I like you a bit, it means you might like me. I hate you at the same time, and my belly hurts when I think about you. Dot hates you, and Dad does. But I still want you to come home and stay.

Why did you leave us for the man? What did I do wrong? Was it when I dropped the cheese? Was it the Dots? Can you tell me so I can fix it and make it all better?

Love from,
Mike/Scamp xxx

"A name," she said, exultation streaming through her. "We've got a bloody name."

Now she wished she hadn't been stubborn and purposely not gone to look. Paul displayed such a smug grin she wanted to punch him. He may as well have said: *Bet you feel all kinds of dickhead now.*

She took her phone out and rang Nada. "Quickly, look at the list of the vans, the ones owned by men."

"Okay, two secs."

Adrenaline joined the exultation, and Tracy felt a bit sick with it. She hauled in a big breath then blew it out slowly, and it calmed her somewhat. "Damon, come and read this. Can you see something I'm missing here? Is there anything there, a hidden meaning?"

He came over and bent close to the sill. Specsavers was in his future. She attempted to read the note again herself, but her mind had scrambled, the words jumbling, and all she could think was Mike, Mike, Mike. How could he have been so stupid as to sign his name? Did he think it was so common he wouldn't be found? Maybe he wouldn't have been had they not known about the van, but they did, and marrying that with the name meant they'd be a giant step closer to arresting the fucker.

"Three are owned by Michaels," Nada said.

"Okay, send me the full names and addresses in a message, because I'm buggered if I'll remember them. Catch you later."

"No, wait!"

"What is it?" Impatience nipped at her. She wanted to get going.

"We've had the forensic report back from Sara's. Dog hair was found, specifically wiry. The suggestions are Border Terrier, Jack Russell, Irish Wolfhound."

She thought back to the magazine picture of a dog left on Sara's sofa. Could it be the same one? "Okay, I'll Google them. Just send me those names and addresses now, we really need them."

"Are we close?"

"Yes, now sod off! You're holding us up." She prodded the End Call button then accessed Google, comparing the dogs on screen with the one drawn on the windowsill and the one in her head from the sofa. The closest was the Irish Wolfhound. Her phone yipped, a bar interrupting her viewing with a notification that Nada had messaged, and she opened it, then replied.

Tracy: IRISH WOLFHOUND. YOU LOT, ALL OF YOU, GET HOLD OF ALL THE VETS. I WANT TO KNOW IF ANYONE CALLED MIKE OR MICHAEL OWNS A DOG

LIKE THAT. WE'RE GOING TO GO AND VISIT THE MEN NOW, SO KEEP YOUR FINGERS CROSSED.

Nada: GO TO THE ONE FOR MICHAEL REDMOND LAST. LARA SAID SHE WENT TO SEE HIM EARLIER, AND HE'S BALD.

Tracy: OKAY.

She didn't continue with: *People do wear wigs and false moustaches, you know.*

"Damon, come on. We have to go."

She rushed downstairs, having a fight with her protective clothing on the doorstep because the bloody suit kept getting tangled in her haste. She resisted screaming—Pam Danridge was just getting into a car with who Tracy assumed was her son, and the woman didn't need the extra upset of Tracy screeching. She battled with the outfit until she'd removed everything and squashed it into an evidence bag by the door. Log signed now an officer stood guard, she darted down the path, wrenching the gate open and speeding through. In the car, she revved the engine, tapping the wheel in frustration while Damon pratted about getting undressed.

She wound down the window. "Hurry up!" God, she could burst. So she didn't explode, she took her phone out and put the details of the first address in the satnav. "Whichever Mike you are, I'm bloody coming for you, sicko."

Damon got in.

"Christ, could you have taken any longer?" She zoomed out of her space and along the street.

"You are one minute away from your destination of shouting at your partner," Damon said in a satnav voice.

"Pack it in. Not funny. I'm so wound up it's unreal."

"I gathered that, but calm down. It's not going to go over well if you turn up at these houses or where they work and—"

"Bollocks. Get hold of Nada for me. I didn't get their work addresses."

He prodded at his phone.

"What did you make of the windowsill message?" she asked.

"Give me a chance! I'm writing to Nada, aren't I." He shook his head.

"Keep your hair on."

"I could say the same for you."

She'd give him that point. "Right. Well. Tell me when you've finished then."

"Just so happens I have. So, we were right. A male child left with his dad. Mother has gone with a new man. Child doesn't like her—so maybe she wasn't too good a parent—yet he then states he likes her a bit. Confused? No clue what the Dots are, but I noticed it was capitalised. We came up blank with the Dorothys in the area, so God knows what it means if it isn't a name. We have dots on their torsos, the dot-to-dot images, so perhaps, with it being capped, the images and dots are important to him."

"No perhaps about it. They *are* important. As are the clues left behind. And what's that about cheese?"

"One of the pictures was a cheese and a knife, don't forget, and a knife image was on Deirdre's stomach."

"So an incident with him dropping cheese, and maybe a knife was involved. Means nothing to us but a lot to him, same as with the Space Raiders and all the rest of it, guaranteed. We're here. This one is Michael Collins. Have you got an answer from Nada yet so we can go straight to his work if he isn't here?"

"Not yet."

"Stay put. Pointless us both getting out if he's not in." She ran up the path and hammered on the door, a bit too enthusiastically, but ho hum. No answer, so she whacked it again with the side of her fist, the silver knocker flapping with the force. The bloody thing was a weird gargoyle.

An old lady came out from next door, another gargoyle, except this one was alive and spitting feathers, not fire or whatever those creatures spewed. "What's all the bashing about, young lady?"

Tracy got out her ID and held it up. "Is he at work?" She jabbed a thumb at the house.

"Yes, and he's abroad for it. Won't be back for a fortnight, been gone the same. I should know, I feed the cat, though why he has one when he's hardly here, I don't know. The poor thing thinks it lives here not there, and I—"

"Thanks!" Tracy turned to leave.

"Rude!" the woman shouted.

I can be a damn sight ruder if you're up for it.

Damon opened the car window. "He's not there!"

"I know that now." She got back in. "Where to?"

"Already sorted the satnav. Just go. Nada sent the info. Michael Collins is in Belgium."

"Right." She drove off, her arms shaking from the rush she always got when they were close to apprehending someone. "Who's next?"

"Michael Bentley. Executive in an office in town." His phone chirruped. "Hold up, another message from Nada."

"Read it out."

"*Michael Redmond is probably our man. He owns an Irish Wolfhound called Dot. I rang his work; boiler engineer—he's off sick.*"

"Fuck me, Dot is a dog! And off sick, my arse. He's off killing, that's what he is. Sort out the new address." Shit, she wanted to pee herself with excitement at the same time as being sick. *Calm down. Get your head in the game.*

"Done it. And I hadn't finished reading the message. The rest says: *Mother, Margaret (Peggy) Redmond, deceased. Murder. Strangulation. Remains found two years after her disappearance inside a hollow log.*"

"Well, bugger me, that fits. So did he strangle her, too?" She flicked her lights on, plus the siren—she'd switch both off once she got closer.

"Hyoid bone was broken."

The drive to this bastard's house was tense, and she had no desire to speak, her mind whirring. Damon knew her of old and kept his mouth shut. She was three streets away now so silenced the siren and killed the blues. One turn, two turns, three, and they were there. No white van out the front, so maybe he wasn't in.

Or maybe he's killing someone else.

She dived from the car and ran up his path, taking a few seconds to steady her breathing and let Damon catch up. Once he stood beside her, she knocked with a knuckle, and a dog barked straight away. She glanced at Damon. He widened his eyes.

ID out, she waited for the door to open.

It didn't.

"The downstairs curtain's just moved," Damon said.

"Right." She knocked again. Opened the letterbox. An Irish Wolfhound stared at her then licked the tips of her fingers, the cheeky bugger. "Michael Redmond, can you come here, please?" She let the flap go. "Now I've got dog spit on me." She wiped her hand on her backside.

"The curtain gap has been closed." Damon sighed. "Shall I go round the back?"

"No, he's coming, look." She nodded at the door, which opened.

"Yes?" A man with a shiny head stood there holding the doggy by the scruff. He had four lines down his cheek, scabbed over.

Victim defence wounds? "Michael Redmond?" she asked.

"Yes..."

"Off to work, are you?"

He glanced at his uniform, one much like a copper's—it had to be him. Elsie Fordenham had said the man at Anne's had this sort of get-up on.

There was a light-brown stain on the white accent at the top of the chest pocket. Food? Old blood?

He blinked. "Um…"

"Only, I thought you were a boiler engineer."

"I am."

"And you go to work dressed like that, do you?"

"I…"

"But you're off sick. At least that's what your boss told us."

He frowned. "Who the bloody hell are you, and how do you know my business?"

She showed him her identification. "DI Tracy Collier and DS Damon Hanks. We need to come in for a bit of a chat."

He licked his teeth, back and forth, back and forth, and his eyes glazed, as if he'd gone into some kind of trance that was a coping mechanism. She'd seen it before and had done the same herself once upon a time.

"Is it about my van again?" he asked.

"Amongst other things."

"But I showed the lady and policeman earlier. There's nothing in there, I assure you." Lick, lick.

"I'll take your word for it." *For now.* "Come on then, let's get the kettle on. We've got quite a lot to talk about. Thirsty work, that is." She didn't want a drink, but it was a way of getting inside. She stepped in, forcing him backwards.

He put the dog in the living room and shut it in, then went towards the kitchen, stopping abruptly in the doorway, his back to them. "Um…err…actually, we'll go in the living room."

"The coffee's not there, though, is it?" she said. "And I'm gasping. Go on, in you go."

He walked in, and Tracy hurried to catch up in case he took it into his head to hide anything. He stood in the dining area, in front of what appeared to be a whiteboard on a tripod. She glanced at the table. A cap on top of a pile of…hair?

"Can you step aside, please, sir?" Damon said.

"I can't." Michael shook his head. "You're not allowed to see the suitcase. It's Peggy's."

The suitcase she used when she left them? "Is that your mother you're talking about? Margaret?"

He nodded, eyes widening so he appeared manic. "Bitch. She's a fucking whore-slapper-bitch."

Christ Almighty, it's definitely him… "Calm down, Mr Redmond. Take a seat, will you?"

"No. You can't tell me what to do anymore, Peggy."

While her hair wasn't the exact shade of all the victims', it was definitely red, and she wondered if he saw her as his mother when she stood beneath a light—that would bring out the red more. She moved to the right and caught sight of the dot-to-dot on the board. Her legs wobbled. "Do you like doing dot-to-dot pictures?"

"Yeah, they make me feel better." He pulled his lips back, curled his tongue over his top teeth, and pressed it down with his fingertips.

Weirdo or what. "Is that a wig there?" She pointed to the table.

He lowered his hand and stared at it for a moment. "It's her hair and moustache." He swiped the cap up and crammed it on, long brown-red hair attached. Then he put the moustache beneath his nose. Only one half stuck, and the other flopped downwards.

If this wasn't so bizarre and creepy, she'd laugh.

"What about what's left on the table?" she asked.

"It's Karma's beard. He's a hairy bastard."

What the fuck? "Okay… What have you been doing since yesterday, sir?"

"I've been with the Peggys."

"How can you be with your mother when she's dead? Do you mean you visited her grave?"

"No. I was at her houses."

Had she owned a lot of property? She'd have to get Nada to look into that. "Did you do anything nice with her?" She got the very real vibe this man was mentally unstable and thought his mother was still alive. She had to be careful how she handled him.

"I…I showed her I'm a winner, not a loser."

"That's lovely. Do you like raw liver, Michael?"

He grabbed the beard and slapped it on his face. It was bushy, and the end reached halfway down his chest. There appeared to be blood on it. "I'm Karma now, with this beard on. Can you see that? You can't touch me like this."

He was getting on her tits. "Answer my question, please."

"No. Hate liver. Hate it like I hate Peggy."

"But don't you like her just a *tinsy* bit?"

"Shut up. You don't know anything."

She tried another angle. "You know when you showed her you were a winner, how did you do that?"

"She's in the bloody log, isn't she. You *know* that. You came here and told us. You're that Nabley woman, and he's Wotton." He jerked his head at Damon.

"No, we're not those people. I think you're confused."

"Don't you tell me what I am or how I feel. You're not me, so how can you know?" He raised a fist.

"Which log? Can you show me?"

He grunted. "No! No one has fags there anymore. It smells. *She* smells. Of rotten meat, they said. They thought it was an animal, and it was. She's an animal. I'm not going back there."

"Where?"

He looked fit to burst. "To the *log*! Haven't you been *listening*, you crazy cow?"

She was crazy? Well, yes, some would say that, but *he* was the insane one here.

She'd had enough now. Time to get to the crux of it. "Look, where's Peggy?"

"In her houses. I left the doors open so she'd be found. Everyone will know what a nasty slag she is now."

A shiver went through her. "Did you kill her, Michael?"

"She deserved whatever she got."

"How many Peggys are there?"

"Six."

Her heart sank. Was there one more out there, or *had* he killed his mother? "I need you to answer my question. Did you kill Peggy?"

"Yes," he hissed, tugging at the cap hair. "See this? I cut it off and put it next to her. Cut it off with the cheese knife."

Bloody hell... She signalled to Damon: *Get the cuffs ready.* He walked to Michael and gently pushed him forward, away from the whiteboard. Michael appeared not to notice. His eyes had gone vacant.

Tracy nodded at Damon, then looked directly at their man. "Michael Redmond, I am arresting you for the murder of Margaret Redmond and the suspected murders of Sara Scott, Olivia Zola, Anne Walton, Deirdre Kaggle, and Rona Danridge. You do not have to say anything, but it may harm your defence if you do not mention when questioned something which you later rely on in court. Anything you do say may be given in evidence."

Damon had cuffed him as she'd spoken, still staring as if he wasn't here but off in his head somewhere.

"Michael," she barked. "Do you understand what I just said?"

He jumped. "Yes. No." He shook his head, and a tear fell, disappearing into the beard. "I don't understand anything. I never have."

CHAPTER TWENTY-ONE

Tracy and Damon sat in one of the viewing rooms, the monitor on the desk in front of them showing Michael and his solicitor, plus a mental healthcare professional, sitting in the soft interview room. Michael had already been through an assessment, and she felt he would reveal more to Zoe Valoutiere, a French lady who specialised in talking to people who'd suffered childhood trauma, instead of her.

Zoe had been living and working in the UK for ten years and was an absolute master at drawing information out. Something about her accent, her calm way of speaking. If Michael wasn't handcuffed, it would appear this was just a chat between friends, but he was, and Quinn stood by the door in case Michael got so distressed he lashed out.

"Here we go," Tracy said. "But I'm not sure I want to hear this." Mainly because she'd spent her childhood embroiled in fear and manipulation, the abuse something no child should go through. She selfishly worried Michael's experience would set her own healing back, but then her job was the sort to bring triggers every step of the way, so if she felt that strongly about it, she should leave.

But she wouldn't. Catching bad people had kept her going since she'd first joined up. She'd be lost without that anchor. She'd be useless at anything else.

"Might be a toughie, granted," Damon said. "The shit he was coming out with at his house—he isn't stable, has gone through too much, I reckon. The way some parents treat their kids... How can you knowingly be cruel and not feel guilty about it? Michael had the potential to be a good man, but look at him. Look at what he's done because of a past he had no control over."

"He's broken."

He still had the cap and hair on, but at his house he'd taken the moustache and wig off, insisting it needed to go into his trouser pocket. They'd allowed that until he'd been placed inside the back of the meat wagon, then Damon had removed them while distracting Michael with a conversation about Dot.

Tracy smiled. They'd visited Wilhelmina Redmond earlier, while Michael was having his assessment. Tracy had broken the news about Michael's arrest and what he'd undoubtedly done, and Wilhelmina had agreed to take Dot, saying her husband would be over the moon about having her. Michael's father suffered from dementia, and while they'd been talking about Michael, the poor man clearly hadn't known who he was, frowning all the while, and saying people who killed ought to be strung up and stoned. He'd added that his wife, Peggy, who'd run away, should also be stoned for killing three dogs, all called Dot.

That explained the cemetery on the picture of the house left at Olivia Zola's. His father must have buried them in the garden at their former family home.

Hopefully, forensics would come through with flying colours and there'd be evidence on the cap hairs, the beard and moustache. And hopefully, that brown stain on the stab vest would be one of the women's blood. There was no way this man had committed all these crimes without taking DNA from the 'Peggys' with him. Tracy didn't really need a full confession. The evidence would speak for them.

"Hello, Michael. My name is Zoe Valoutiere, and I'd like to talk to you about Peggy."

He stared at her as if measuring her up, then immediately launched into a story, one that gradually revealed the clues he'd left behind, and Tracy's chest hurt with the heaviness his childhood put there. She couldn't help but feel sorry for him, but also for the women he'd killed, who'd done nothing but have the same hair colour as his mother.

"What about the clothes you had on when the police came to your house?" Zoe asked gently.

"I can't remember that far back. Who remembers all those years ago?" He tutted.

"I'm sorry, perhaps we have our wires crossed. Which years?"

He narrowed his eyes. "When Nabley and Wotton came to say Peggy was in the log."

"My apologies for not being clear. I don't mean then. I mean today. You had a uniform on. What is that for?"

"I issue High Court writs."

"I see. Why do you do that?"

His solicitor wrote that down.

Michael told her about the bailiffs coming round regarding a loan his mother had fraudulently taken out, then explained they'd had to go and live with his nan. "So I put the uniform on, make a writ, then go to Peggy's house to let her know how it felt to be scared when two men come in and take your stuff, and all because of what she'd done. Except it's not two men, it's just me."

"I can understand how you wish to make her feel the same things you did. Is that why you did what you did to Sara, Olivia, Anne, Deirdre, and Rona?"

"That's not their names. They're Peggys."

"Can you explain what the six dolls mean on your mantelpiece?"

"They're all Peggys!" he shouted. "All her, in her stupid skirt."

"About that skirt. That was also in your house. How did you come to have it?"

"I took it off her. By the log."

"Tell me about the black bin liner that was found in your cupboard under the stairs. Why is there a boiler suit in it, covered in blood?"

"Because her arm got sliced, and the blood went everywhere. I didn't want it on me."

"Did you put the suit on before her wrist was sliced?"

"Yes."

"Why?"

"Because I just did." Michael appeared uncomfortable. Under the microscope.

Tracy sighed. *She's aiming for the premeditation angle. Pointless. We know he planned everything. He doesn't need to admit that.*

Zoe kept stock still. "Let's move along. I can see you're getting agitated. Do you collect things, Michael? Is that maybe a hobby you enjoy?"

"I don't know." He shrugged, sticking his bottom lip out.

"I think hobbies are wonderful. I believe you do like collecting because you have a lot of dot-to-dot books stored under the bed in your spare room.

Some look old, as though you've kept them from since you were a child. Is that right?"

"Yes, I love them. Not the compass, though. I don't love that. Peggy stole my first one, and Dad had to buy another. She stabbed the Dots with it. And she strangled them until they were gone."

"Which Dots are those?"

"My *dogs*! God, are you thick?" He rocked his head back and forth sharply as though nutting an imaginary wall. Perhaps he thought it was the proverbial brick one because Zoe's questions were getting to him.

"We'll move on. That spare bedroom. Why is it decorated for a lady? There's flowery wallpaper and pink curtains."

"It's like what Peggy had with my dad. Before she left. They had a bedroom just like that, but I couldn't fit a double bed in because it's too small. The room, I mean. I put Peggy in there, and she had the Aztec material round her mouth. She woke up, and I asked her about the suitcase, but she kept saying she wasn't Peggy, lying to me, so I had to shut her up."

"Did you recreate your parents' bedroom, or was it already like that when you moved into your present house?"

"Yes, I did it all by myself. Olivia helped me. She was my girlfriend until she finished with me on Sunday. She left me just like Peggy did."

Zoe nodded in apparent sympathy. "Back to your collection hobby, Michael. You have a lot of toothbrushes. Do you like those as much as you like the dot-to-dot books?"

"Peggy shouldn't have taken hers. She should have stayed, even though I was scared of her, even though I wanted her to go. But I wanted her to stay, too, and she didn't. She walked out, over the glass, and kicked Dot, and Dad told her right off." He licked his teeth.

Got to be something he does as a soothing action. Tracy sighed again. "I don't think I want to listen anymore."

"Hang on, I missed what Zoe just said." Damon put a hand on Tracy's knee, which meant: *Shut up*.

"I just wanted it there, the toothbrush. If it was there, then it meant she might have come back," Michael said. "And I wanted her blood everywhere, so she'd always be there—a part of her would, because she'd taken her clothes and toothbrush. Then I could cuddle it when I got lonely."

"Cuddle the blood or the toothbrush?" Zoe asked.

"The blood!" He tugged at the cap hair.

"But how can you cuddle blood when it's in Sara's house? You won't be allowed to go there anymore."

"Stop talking," Michael snapped. "I've had just about enough of this shit." He snatched the cap off. "I need to get home to Dot. She'll be missing me."

"Dot is with your dad." Zoe carefully reached across and slid the cap behind her.

They needed it for evidence, and Michael had protested at giving it up earlier.

He sighed as if Zoe was a bit dense. "He can't bloody care for her! He has dementia."

"Don't worry yourself. Wilhelmina will feed your dog and take her for walks, she said so. She hopes you're okay, Michael, and she sends her love."

Tears fell at that. "How can she love me when my own mum didn't?" He rocked his head again. "And Dot will wonder where I've gone. Look, how long have we got left here? I want to go home."

Tracy whispered, "Does he not remember what he's just told us? And that he *can't* go home? Do you think he's been in some sort of place in his head, and now he's back as himself again?"

"Shh!" Damon said.

Zoe sat forward and clasped her knees. "Do you remember being arrested, Michael?"

"This is all bollocks."

"Did you kill all the Peggys?"

"There's more of them to go yet. I need to get to the others." He went to put the cap and hair back on. Frowned. Patted around in search of it. "Where's Mum's hair? What have to done with her hair?"

Tracy stood. "That's it, no more for me."

Damon got up and opened the door. "You go on and get yourself a coffee. I want to watch it all."

She left and went upstairs to the incident room and made two coffees while her team quietly worked behind her. She took the cups to Winter's office, unable to get the images out of her head that Michael's story had conjured. That poor kid, under the bed a lot with his puppies. And as for his mother killing them—what sort of monster was she?

Sighing to let all the emotion out, she tapped Winter's door with her foot.

"Come in."

And she did, preparing herself to go through it all over again.

Lovely.

Printed in Great Britain
by Amazon